OTHER BOOKS BY ELICK MOLL:

Night Without Sleep (1950)
Seidman and Son (1958)
Memoir of Spring (1961)

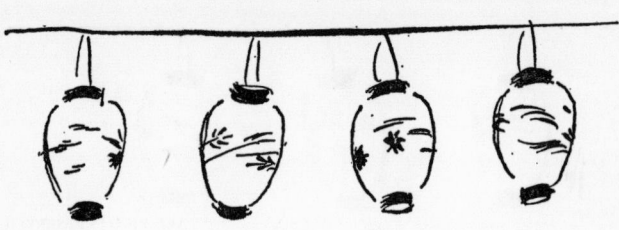

MR. SEIDMAN
and the Geisha

BY ELICK MOLL

DRAWINGS BY FRED BANBERY

SIMON AND SCHUSTER

NEW YORK 1962

LIBRARY OF CONGRESS CATALOG CARD NUMBER: 62–14281
MANUFACTURED IN THE UNITED STATES OF AMERICA
BY THE BOOK PRESS, BRATTLEBORO, VT.

For Robert, Arlene and Andrea

MR. SEIDMAN

and the Geisha

Well, my writer friend, what do you think, I became such a world traveler since I saw you last? Japan, Israel, Greece, Italy—we were away nearly three months. Marvelous experience, the whole thing. But Japan especially. What a country. If I were a young man like you—well, what's the use talking?

So tell me, how's things in California? What's with the movie business? Still dying, at a big profit? I see that you still got your beautiful tan, regardless. Could I ask you a question, you wouldn't get insulted? You think if you and your colleagues were a little paler the movies would be maybe a little better? All right, I'm an old friend, I'm entitled to one little joke. It's anyway in the family, you know I am a big movie fan, from way back.

The trip? Partly business, partly pleasure. I made a connection with a firm in Osaka—Nakamura—maybe you heard of it, very big manufacturer, makes a beautiful line of print fabrics. I think it will work out to very good advantage for the business.

Don't worry about my time. I've got nothing but time. Since my son joined me here in the business, I had to hire a secretary to find me something to do. So make yourself comfortable, we'll have a nice talk. Could I send down for something for you, a sandwich, a drink, something? Oh here, you want to try something a little different, try one of these. Tea cakes. They're imported, from Kyoto. I see you got your eye on the box. Beautiful thing, no? It's also Japanese. You know what it was originally? You couldn't guess. A make-up box. For a geisha. It's very old, maybe a couple of hundred years. I got no idea what it's worth, I didn't buy it, it's a present. What story? Somebody made me a gift, must there be a story? Suppose I would tell you a name, O-yuki. Would you know more than you knew before?

All right, don't be a nag. Forget you're a writer for one afternoon. Take a bite of that cake already. What do you say? Delicious, no? But delicate, like a whisper got turned into a taste. You like that expression. Sure, sure, I've got the soul of an artist. Don't ever say this to my creditors, please, they'll start closing in on me.

I got other secrets I keep from them. Like sometimes on a slack day I sneak away, go down to Fourth Avenue, around Twelfth Street, where there's all the secondhand book shops, and I'll spend there a few hours rummaging around. Since I was a kid I always had the feeling there's gold mines stuck away on those shelves. You know, I got an idea the inside of my head must look something like inside those stores? What I didn't stuff in there over the years. Was always a passion with me, the reading. Like some men want to sleep with every woman in the world, I wanted to read every book. Every new author, it was like a love affair. All of Jack London, all of O. Henry, Mark Twain, Victor Hugo, Balzac, Tolstoy—but with the modern stuff I had to give up finally, resign myself I couldn't swallow it all before I die. Still, even now, it's not a pastime with me. More like a dope addiction. I couldn't sit two minutes in a barber chair, for instance, or a bath, without a book. And going to bed, this is entirely out of the question. You know, I fixed up in my library a few years ago a couch I could use when I want to read late. My sister Bessie heard about it, she started wringing her hands, what kind of a calamity struck the family, what's going on, what came between me and Sophie? I felt like telling her Marjorie Morningstar, but the way she is, she would start looking right away for her address, to send her a lawyer letter.

But if you are mentioning my artistic soul already, I got to tell you it's true I turned down quite a few other possibilities to become a dress manufacturer. When I was a boy, for instance, I wanted the worst way to give Heifetz a little competition on the violin. Then I remember, I had once an idea I would like to be an art critic, like that fellow Berenson, live in a Florentine garden and have every morning Michelangelo or Rembrandt for breakfast. And just lately came to me an idea that maybe I've got a very big talent to be a beachcomber. Who could tell if I made the right choice? One thing I could tell you, if I would have gone into some other line, like collecting shells on the beach in Tahiti, or finding where the elephants go to die in Africa, I don't think now I would be dreaming about what a lovely life I could have had in the dress business.

My impressions of Japan? In which way? No, I don't mind talking about it. I don't know where you got the idea I'm being closemouthed with you. You've certainly got the right customer, I've only been talking my head off to you for years. But I'm just afraid I shouldn't sound like a damn fool. I spent altogether four weeks in the country and now I'm going to give in my showroom, afternoons, lectures on the subject. Like I would be Columbus—he was looking for spices, I was looking to make a connection for textiles, he discovered America and I discovered Japan.

It's such a ridiculous thing. I heard already,

people go to a strange country, they don't know the history, they don't speak the language, they talk to hotel clerks and shopkeepers and guides and other tourists, they stay for six days, the last day they've got nothing to see any more, they ran out of attractions, and they come back home, they are authorities. They can tell you about the political situation, how the people feel about the UN, about Communism, about Marilyn Monroe and President Kennedy, also where to get the bargains, where to get a good corned beef sandwich in Tokyo —me, I'm not an authority. I am only a man who feels very lucky in his life to make the acquaintance of a wonderful, fascinating country. And not the sights, the architecture. The people. They got a hold on me someway, I don't know how I could explain it to you.

Take the little shop in Kyoto where I bought those tea cakes. It's two by four, the man makes them himself, by hand, the same way his great-grandfather did, and he puts them in a box for you, like he's designing a piece of jewelry or a tapestry or something. He doesn't know about the factories, the cheap copies, the pachinko parlors, nothing. This is not his Japan, this is a mishmash, came flying out like from Pandora's box, when that Admiral sailed in there a hundred years ago and opened it up, like they say. What he knows, when you pay him, he bows, like he would be apologizing that he's got to take the money, and he gives you with the cakes a paper with some Buddhist saying on it, and he tells you, for the guide to translate, that if you eat these cakes, and keep your heart pure, you will live long and prosper. And this is not like the bald barber who's selling you a miracle hair tonic. This man is himself maybe ninety years old, maybe more.

Anyway, I left with him a standing order to send me, every month, a supply. What can I lose? Even if they only keep me going until eighty, I still figure it's a good investment. But you should hear my sister Bessie on this subject. You remember I've got a sister Bessie, God bless her, every time she comes in for a fitting I am fixed up with a heartburn for a week. So last time I gave her one of these tea cakes to taste. She makes a face and spits it out.

"What is it?" she says. I tell her it's a Japanese pastry and it's made only of very healthy ingredients.

"Pastry?" she says. "Tastes like paper. And not even first quality paper." And then she has to give me a dig. "What's the matter, you have to go to Japan to get your pastry? Strudel isn't good enough for you? Pretty soon, you became such an international character, you wouldn't be able to put a piece of halvah in your mouth if it doesn't come from a little shop in Constantinople."

Well, it's all according your nature, you see. One person could come away from Japan and he's only disgusted with all the bowing, he remembers those ambassadors in Washington, how they were bowing and smiling all over the place six hours before Pearl Harbor, and he's got the impression it's only sneaky and false, all this show of courtesy. Another person could feel, the way I do, that the people there had nothing to do with the war, except to get killed from it and suffer from it, like they've always done with war, and poverty, and typhoons, and earthquakes. I don't know which is the truth. I could just tell you I was very touched by these people. I got from them, I don't know, such a feeling how they appreciate life, beauty, nature—but quiet, always quiet. You come into a room, there's one flower in a vase, not five dozen. One picture on a wall, not a whole roomful, one on top of another, you have to get on a ladder to see.

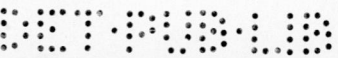

But again, you take my sister Bessie, she doesn't understand this. If one picture is good, why shouldn't six be better? If she takes a bite of something and it doesn't explode in her mouth, like a piece of pickled herring or a knish filled with pepper, it's no good. Tastes like paper. All right, let her live and be well. But to me it was a big revelation, a whole new style of living.

Well, I'll give you a for instance. We were staying in Miyanoshita . . . Who's we? Who do you think? My wife and me. Listen, I can see you are still sniffing around for a story. I told you and please, for heaven's sake, relax. I didn't leave in Japan a Madame Butterfly or a girl on the dock saying, *Sayonara,* Seidman-san. You're smiling, ha?

You remember yourself, one day I sat down with you on a bench in Central Park, you asked me a couple of questions, like now, very polite, very interested, and I answered you. And a year later I wake up, I'm a household word on Seventh Avenue. Morris Seidman—Dior to the masses.

Why should I mind? You gave me a very fine character in the book. I wish I would be more like him. Thank you for the good opinion. Maybe I could tell you a few things would change your mind about me. Anyway, I started to say, we went one day for an excursion to Fuji, that's the mountain with the snow, you see it in all the postcards. Well, we were surrounded that day by hundreds of school kids. Everywhere we went, actually, it was the same thing. The Japanese are peculiar people, they like to see the sights in their own country and they like the children should see too. Not like here in New York. You couldn't drag either the kids or the parents to the Statue of Liberty with a derrick. It's corny. What isn't corny these days? Very little. Sentiment, poetry, emotion, respect—all corny. You want to be on the safe side? Sit in the coffeehouse, listening to Fabian on the jukebox. The great operatic tenor. Some advertisement for Young America. You could cry, honest to God.

Anyway, it was very nice, Fuji, what you could see in the fog. I'll tell you the truth, I'm not such a bug on scenery. There's plenty of mountains in this country, bigger ones, that I never would go out of my way to see. What is interesting to me is people, how they are living, different ways, different ideas. The kids crowding around, with their eyes like swatches of suède, they only want you to take their pictures, or talk to them in English. But the old people, there's more than just the age standing between them and the youngsters—when you lift the camera they turn away. I can understand. The foreigner took away their country, never mind business is better than ever, the wages are higher. What they lost they will never get back again.

Well, we were coming back to Miyanoshita, it was a big trip, a long day, we were tired, sleepy, it was maybe eleven, twelve o'clock at night, and I see from the taxi a black figure standing on the side of the road, looking out at the fields and talking to somebody, but the somebody isn't there. It's a funny feeling, you know, a strange country, a person stands like a shadow in the road, you think maybe it's not really a person, maybe you saw a ghost or something. I lean over to the driver, he's also our guide, and I ask him. So he says, yes, it's a woman, he knows her, her name is Yoriko. So what is she doing, standing in the road, in the

middle of the night, talking to herself? She's not talking, he says. She's singing. She's a farm woman and she's singing to the rice, they planted it a little while ago. Can you imagine? Every night she comes out and sings to the rice. Like to a baby, a lullaby, it should sleep well, grow straight and healthy, have a fine character.

All right, this is just one little thing. Another for instance. You go to a party here, it's either for a birthday, or a celebration, or a *bar mitzvah,* or just to drink too much and eat too much and say the same things you said a hundred times before to the same people. Did you ever hear somebody should make a party, in the spring, and it's for insect-hearing? I mean it. An insect-hearing party. People come together and they sit in the garden, drink a little tea and listen to the insects. Or else, if there is a moon, could be a moon-viewing party. Am I peculiar, to fall in love with people for this? To me an insect was only something you hit with a fly swatter, or you put citronella on your arms, or you went around spraying kerosene on the bed-springs. I would like to be the kind of person, live the kind of life, where I would give insect-hearing parties. My misfortune is my friends would only think I'm crazy, not that I turned into a philosopher. What they want to hear at my house is the riffle from a pinochle deck.

But by myself, here in the office, I have sometimes a little tea in the afternoon now. Not in a glass. Japanese tea, the way they do it, with a little ceremony. To make the mind quiet, think quiet thoughts. Sometimes I go for lunch to a restaurant on Sixth Avenue, serves Japanese food. When the girl comes to take my order she bows. I bow back. I sit on a cushion on the floor, it's a little hard on the knees at my age but I enjoy it, the whole atmosphere. Reminds me of the trip.

I tell you, I wish I had the nerve, I would wear a kimono here in the office sometimes. Of course, this would create quite a commotion if the delegate from the union, for instance, would decide he wants to have an argument with me just then, how I am oppressing the workers. Or Mr. Bernstein from the Monarch Silk Company. I could just see their faces. This Bernstein's been trying for a couple of years anyway to get me to take from his analyst. A man my age, he says, has got to have problems. Just because I don't show anything is no sign I don't need help. Could be going on inside, all the tensions building up and one day, bang, there's a coronary thrombosis, or I'm in jail for pinching a girl on the subway. Happens I don't ride the subway but maybe he's right, in general. Maybe this is a significant thing, I came down suddenly with a kimono complex.

I could just see my sister Bessie if she came in the office and I'm sitting here in a kimono. Can you imagine? You should hear her anyway if I dare to open my mouth to say a good word for Japan or the Japanese. She's on me like a tiger. How is it I forgot so quick about Pearl Harbor? What am I, a traitor or something? Until now, she says, whenever they needed for a movie or a mystery story a real villain, the best would be a Japanese, five feet one inch tall, with thirty-six teeth instead of thirty-two, and glasses, and what was inside those kimono sleeves, you would get shivers thinking about it. Now comes Marlon

Brando in a movie, with some Japanese floozies with slanty eyes and fedora hats, standing on a bridge, and all of a sudden all of Brooklyn is steaming into the Imperial Hotel, like Commodore Perry into Yokohama Harbor and all over Flatbush it's nothing but kimonos and shoji screens and Mikimoto pearls and bonsai plants, and what about all the girls who disappear off the streets and end up white slaves in Hong Kong?

You think it's any use to tell her Hong Kong is not Japan? I'm better off to keep my mouth shut. If she knew what really happened to me there in Japan . . . well, have another tea cake and tell me what's with you? How's the writing business? How's the love life out there in Hollywood?

No, I'm not teasing you. I guess I'm self-conscious, actually. Listen, what's the use of your making me promises you wouldn't write any of this down? You remind me, I had a cousin once, Simon, couldn't stay away from the booze. He's dead, poor fellow. But I remember how he would say to me that this time the money I'm going to give him, *if* I'll give him, it's going for rent and shoes for the baby, not one drink, not even a smell, honest to God. I knew it was only a question how many saloons he would be able to pass. Three,

four, six, but sooner or later you give a look, the
doors are swinging and Simon is gone. The same
thing with you. Absolutely, you say, this is between
you and me, you wouldn't write down a word.
But you are a writer. I know whatever I'll tell you
here will be burning a hole in your pocket. You'll
be sitting one day at the typewriter, you'll say to
yourself, what's the harm? One little story? If
you'll change around the names, the incidents,
like before, nobody will recognize it, nobody will
be hurt—and goodbye Charlie with the promises.
Chapter One—Seidman and the Geisha.

Yes, that's what I said. Listen, hold yourself in
a little, for God's sake. You are like a bloodhound,
you got the smell of the victim in your nose, you
can't wait to gobble me up. No, I'm only joking.
Like I said, I'm feeling self-conscious, even with
you. I'm wondering, should I talk about what happened, or shouldn't I?

You know, I am not a worldly man. I mean, in one respect. I suppose most men my age had at least a few experiences with women. Maybe because I didn't, I exaggerate the whole thing. I mean, it's not that I'm completely an idiot and I don't know what goes on. Thirty years in the dress business, it's not like I would have spent them in a nunnery, all the ladies come boxed up like starch. I've got models running in and out of my showroom the whole day, even if I don't look very hard I've got to see sometimes that there's other women in the world besides my Sophie got a pretty bust and a cute behind. And whatever I couldn't pick up for myself, my star salesman, Larry, is always Johnny on the spot to give me an education, the latest thing in sex. And I don't sit in judgment. I am not shocked, for instance, to see a lodge member of mine the other day, in a certain hotel, walks up to the desk with a young girl and a suitcase, I know it's empty. So let him live and be well. Maybe for him, he needs it. I just know for me, I couldn't do it. Not that I'm from wood. I could get you an affidavit for this from my Sophie. If she wouldn't slap my face. I guess we are pretty old-fashioned in this respect. Even with the children, this department we keep strictly private. I don't know if it's good. This is how we are and I don't want to change it. Maybe it's just that I was always afraid. In my day, they put such a fright into you, what could happen with sex, all kinds of terrible things, you would get blind, your children would be blind, your brains would turn to mush—maybe I got from this an inhibition or something.

You know, I had a couple of propositions in my life, believe it or not. Models—one time a buyer from—well, I wouldn't tell you where. Only it was the South. We were in my office, this was seven, eight years ago, I remember it like yesterday. We were finished with business, I got from her that day a very nice order and we were sitting, talking. She was actually an educated girl—well, girl, she was maybe thirty-eight—but with a college degree, and no fool, believe me. She talked very nice, a little bit with molasses on the words, the way they do in the South, I'm not too fond of it, actually, but this woman, it fitted very well with her personality and she discussed, very intelligent, about conditions in the South and about William Faulkner. I remember, she mentioned how he understood the South better than anybody. Maybe he does but I'll tell you the truth, I can't understand him. I'm not used to start a sentence on page two and it finishes on page seven. And the South, for my part, I don't want to understand it. I just want they should let go already, this terrible thing. A crime against nature.

Anyway, we were talking, I didn't realize it was closing time till my production man puts his head in the door and says good night, he's closing up and am I coming to the Turkish Bath tonight. So I said that I got a little work to do in the shop, I would decide later. And when the door closes, she gives me a peculiar look, then she puts her hand on my arm and she says, "How do you keep in condition? Golf?"

So I say to her, "What condition? I got a rubber tire around my middle, you could run a small tractor on it."

And she says, "Never mind, you're very muscular," and she runs her hand now around my chest. I'm getting a little nervous, maybe she wants me to return the compliment, and this is a game I never learned how to play.

So I want to put her off, change the mood, I say to her, "Whatever muscles I've got, I developed them sweeping out the feathers from the poultry store in front where we lived, on Delancey Street."

She laughs, and she says, "You are the cutest man," and then she leans over and gives me a kiss. And then she says, plain, like we would be talking about how many tucks to put in a pleated skirt, "You know, Morris, I've been wanting to go to bed with you for four years and I learned in school that to every action there must be an equal and opposite reaction. How would you like to take me to dinner, something light, like a dozen oysters and a bucket of champagne and maybe I'll get a little tight and drop my hotel key in your pocket."

I swear to you, the very words. I remember like they would have been carved on my shaking knees. The last thing I expected was a proposition from this woman. Or any woman, to tell you the truth.

Was I tempted? What, tempted? All I was thinking was how could I get out of this predicament. First of all, she's a good customer, I could count on her every season for a substantial order, and I don't want to lose the business. But more important is that, no matter how I will say it, how diplomatic I'll try to be, if my answer is no, she's going to be humiliated. And this is not some tramp, this is a woman with pride, from a good family, I can't push a *No* in her face, like a wet mop.

So I figure, time. I've got to have time, maybe something will turn up, an inspiration, some solution. I say to her, "Agnes—" this is not her right name and listen, when you are writing, please don't change it because maybe by accident you'll hit on the right one—"Agnes," I say, "I won't waste time making you a speech, how you took the words out of my mouth. Let's better talk about where we should go for the oysters."

Well, to make a long story short, God is good sometimes. I don't know if it was the champagne, I'm not much of a drinker, or the oysters, or both together, or because I was so nervous, anyway, we get to her hotel, I got sick. But I mean sick.

"You look kind of green," she says to me. "Maybe you need some black coffee, I'll send down for some."

"I think I need to be excused," I said and I went in the bathroom. I didn't want to make a mess so I kneeled down by the toilet and put my arms around, like it would be my long-lost uncle from Bialystok, and that was the end of my problem with Agnes. Lucky she didn't have to call the manager to get my head out of the bowl.

Isn't it amazing, the things that can happen in a lifetime? Even to ordinary people. I sit here in my office sometimes and I think: Kyoto. Gion. Pontocho. And I wonder, was I really there, in a street with little houses and lanterns in front, like a child's dream? Did I really meet there, me, Morris Seidman, a girl whose name means Honorable Moon Child? Must be I dreamed this, or I got mixed up for a while in somebody else's story, like in those plays by that Italian you gave me to read, Pirandello.

Well, you got me started now, like always, so I'm going to tell you. You can cancel your other appointments. You wanted to hear, all right, you'll sit here now until I tell you the whole thing, from the beginning.

First of all, you know how I've been talking all these years about making a trip to Italy. This was my dream. So why the other direction entirely, to Japan, when I made up my mind to make a trip, finally? Well, came about this way. We had last year a big success with a style we made up from Thai silk. You know what it is? It's from Bangkok, hand-loomed, very beautiful material, beautiful shades. I make a popular-priced line, which you know, and ordinarily this would be too expensive for me, the material, with the duty and everything. But this was a job lot, ten thousand yards, and the broker offered it to me at a very good price. The only thing he said his client doesn't want cash. He wants instead a shipment of Welsbach mantles. You remember them? They stopped making them maybe thirty years ago, more. Well, seemed peculiar and I was curious the name of the client. The broker tells me it's the Shanghai Trading Company in Tokyo.

I must tell you about this firm. Very interesting. The Shanghai Trading Company was started sixty years ago by a Ukrainian Jew, his name is Ruditzky, he's over eighty years old now and he's still sharp as a razor. A real genius with a *draydle*. You don't know what this is. Well, I'll explain it to you. Take beaver hats. This was once a very big business in this country, they sold them everywhere, Europe, all over. Astor made a fortune. So say this Ruditzky hears that beaver hats are all of a sudden out of style, a drug on the market, the whole industry is collapsing. It actually happened like this, overnight. So he buys up a couple of shiploads of beaver hats for a song and he finds a market, in Lapland for instance. But he can't get money there because they haven't got money. But reindeers they've got. So he takes for the beaver hats four shiploads of reindeer meat and this he sells to a company in the Fiji Islands, they haven't got meat but they've got copra and whales. He gets for the reindeers three shiploads of copra and three of dried blubber, what's left after they cook out the oil from the whales. The copra he puts in a warehouse for next year's *draydle,* and the blubber he sells to a farmers' collective in Peoria, Illinois, it's very good for fertilizer. But again he doesn't take money, he takes wheat. Not wheat that they have now in the granary but what they'll grow later, from the fertilizer. And this he sells, futures, on the Johannesburg Commodity Market and he takes instead of money, shares in the African Development Company which five years later are worth five million dollars. This is a *draydle*.

He piled up like this, in the old days, an enormous fortune in Shanghai. The Communists took it away from him but he started up again in Tokyo and now he's got offices all over Asia, he's got a couple of sons educated in America, a dozen grandchildren scattered around in the business, but the old man still keeps his hands on the throttle, nobody makes a move without him.

All this I didn't find out about until later. Meanwhile I wanted the silk, it was a very good buy, but where am I going to get him Welsbach mantles? Eventually I got him instead a hundred thousand rolls of some kind of wire netting, it's probably keeping out mosquitoes or lizards in Indonesia somewhere.

But in the meantime we got into quite a correspondence. I've got tremendous respect for these characters—you know, they come to a foreign

country, without money or connections, most times not even an education, and just with their ingenuity they build up a fortune. Me? Don't be foolish, I am not even in a class with Ruditzky. I must tell you sometime about an uncle of mine, came to this country with a parcel, there was in it a couple of handkerchiefs and half a salami from the trip in steerage, and he started in a basement on Second Avenue, a business melting off the silver from the back of old photographic plates and selling it to dentists and jewelers— well, this is another story.

Anyway, I got from this old man Ruditzky one day a letter, he suggested I should come to Tokyo for a visit. It would be to my advantage, he says, he'll see to it. He'll introduce me to the Jewish

community there and also to some Japanese manu-
facturers, textiles and so on, he's sure I can make
a valuable connection. Besides, he's going to have
an eightieth birthday and I could congratulate
him, personally.

Well, this is all my son Harold has to hear. He
starts to nag me, why don't I go. "Why don't you
take Mom and go for a real trip? Around the world
maybe. A second honeymoon."

So I say, "We didn't have our first yet. We
went right from the ceremony to a flat in the
Bronx. We had our wedding breakfast in the Automat. A Vienna roll for a nickel and a cup of
coffee."

He gives me a big grin and puts an arm around
my shoulder and says, "Pop, why are you re-
minding me all the time of what a tough time
you had? You want me to move to the Bronx
and ride the subway to the shop? And eat in the
Automat?"

My children, you know, are always giving me
a little something to think about, just in case I
should maybe puff myself up with the idea I did
a pretty good job with them. It's kind of fresh,
what he said, but could be there's some truth in
it. We parents are always imagining that every-

thing we did was for the children, even to create them in the first place. We don't want them to make the same mistakes we did, to have to struggle like we did, and so on. Still and all, when it comes right down to it, may be we resent a little, too, how easy we made it for them, everything falls into their laps, and all they have to do is holler they want to be independent and where's my socks.

Well, I don't know, my wife is the psychologist in the family and she is welcome to it. From me, Mr. Freud would never have made a living. But what I wanted to tell you, you remember when Harold came into the business finally, he decided he wasn't cut out to be a writer and he was going to buckle down and follow in my footsteps? He made me then a speech, how much he admired me, I was a genius in my line and he only hoped he could begin, in five years, ten years, to know enough to take the burden off my shoulders a little.

I said to myself then, wait. One year and he'll start pushing me out. Well, it didn't take a year. The first thing, he wants me to join a club, play golf a couple of afternoons a week. Then, you know, I can never hear too much music, so Harold says this is my golden opportunity to catch up, there's afternoons always a recital somewhere and Friday the Symphony Orchestra, and so on. If I put my mind to it I could find something every day of the week to take me away from the shop.

"Why not?" Harold says. "You're getting along, Pop. You ought to start taking it a little easy."

Getting along. Anybody who is over thirty is already in a decline with these kids. "You've put in your time," he says. "You're entitled to relax a bit."

"And if I relax," I say, "maybe I'll live to a ripe old age of fifty-five?"

Anybody would be listening, they've got to say, "What a darling boy, such a considerate son." He only wants his Pop to take it a little easy, slacken off a little, save himself, not overstrain, go to afternoon concerts, play a little golf, join a club, take a vacation, go on a honeymoon. But the main thing, believe me, is Pop should disappear, make himself scarce, get lost, give him some elbowroom so he can spread out and take over the business, show what he can do without the old fogy around.

So what's the upshot? I went away finally for a few months, what do I find when I get back? Calamity. My worst fears. We are getting more business than ever, the customers are happy, the government is happy, we are making more profit than ever. The only thing got ruined was my little fantasy this business couldn't get along without me. Proud? Of course I'm proud. Who wouldn't be? A boy twenty-four years old comes into a business, and in a year's time he's got such a grasp of the whole operation, you wouldn't believe it. Still and all, gives you a little squeeze too, you realize something you put practically your whole life into it, and now a bright boy could take it away from you with his left hand. No, I'm not exaggerating. You should see some of the innovations he put in here, behind my back. Of course, he got a little help from IBM too.

Anyway, it's decided we are going. Well, Marco Polo made also a trip to the Orient. But he didn't take along my Sophie. First the shots. Smallpox and typhoid fever you must take. But Sophie figures, on the same piece of lemon, why shouldn't we take everything they've got? After all, you only have to meet one unfriendly germ and the whole trip is ruined. So I am now immune to bubonic plague, diphtheria, polio, lockjaw, yellow fever, cholera, sleeping sickness—they couldn't find on me any more room where to put the needle.

Then comes the luggage. You know, my wife, ordinarily, is a very sensible woman. But in this situation it's like she suddenly lost her reason. I explain to her ten times, we are planning a trip that will cost us maybe fifteen, twenty thousand dollars. This is all right with her, but the sixty-six pounds of luggage we're allowed free on the plane, this is the place where she is going to save money. I'm telling you, it practically spoiled the whole trip for us. Three weeks she was packing and unpacking, putting in and taking out. Four times I had to go to Altman's for suitcases, maybe five hundred dollars' worth, all sizes, shapes, fold up, stand up, hang up—incidentally, we didn't use one. Not one. We used the old suitcases, from going to the mountains.

Every night, I come home from the shop, there's no time to eat dinner. I've got to try out the new arrangement with the suitcases. She's standing in the bedroom, all the closets and drawers are emptied onto the bed, and she looks like Lady Macbeth, the hair rumpled, the eyes wild, and I got to take the suitcases and go stand on the bathroom scale, on and off, on and off, the whole night long. Comes time to go to bed we are exhausted, we're not talking to each other. Should she take this, should she leave that, what if it rains, what if it's cold, what if it's hot—and the biggest worry of all, God forbid we should run out of soap and toilet paper in the middle of Japan.

No use to reason with her. I said to her, "Sophie, for heaven's sake, you are taking all the pleasure out of this trip before we even start. Where do you think we are going? To a jungle? The Japanese are the greatest makers of things in the world. They *invented* toilet paper and soap. And I would rather use leaves already and let's make an end with this packing and unpacking. You look like a wreck," I said. "I bet you lost ten pounds."

It's true, we're going for our first trip abroad, ought to be a big excitement for us and it's like there would have been a death in the family or something.

"What is it?" I said. "It's going to cost us so much, suppose we'll spend another few hundred dollars for overweight? Is this a reason to get a nervous breakdown?" So she sits down on the bed, in the middle of a mountain of lingerie, and she starts to cry.

"Why don't *you* pack?" she says. "Why don't *you* lift a finger to get us prepared for the trip? You're all day in the shop, making big decisions. Why don't you make one here? No, criticize. I'm the flunky and all you can do is criticize. I'm not going," she says. "You go. Do your own packing. You didn't want me along in the first place," she says.

Well, this is logical, no? I went to Harold, I told him, "The trip is canceled. We're not going."

"What happened?" he says. "I thought everything was all set. Ruditzky is expecting you, he made reservations at the Imperial for you, he's got a whole schedule planned—"

"Well, it's no use," I say. "Your mother doesn't want to go."

"But why?"

"Why? Because she can't find a suitcase to put in fifteen winter dresses, fourteen summer dresses, six evening dresses, seven suits, twelve pairs of shoes, thirty-seven pounds of toilet articles, four umbrellas, twenty rolls of toilet paper and a case of soap, should weigh just sixty-six pounds."

Anyway, to make a long story short, we're on the plane finally, we said goodbye to the children, I managed to find a place to put away a few things Sophie figured we got to have on board—a toilet case, a zipper case, an attaché case, two packages of books, a few coats, a utility bag, a shoe bag—why a *shoe* bag, for God's sake?—well, by now I'm not

asking any questions, because any minute will come one from which we got to get a divorce altogether.

Well, finally we are going down the runway, flying, but still on the ground, you know what terrific power these jets have got, it's too much already. I was thinking how I was running after my Harold on a bicycle when he was learning to ride, and I was worried he's growing up in a world where there's too much speed—well, I'm glad I remembered to take care of everything, the will and so on. And just then I hear Sophie say, like she would be tuned in, "Did you remember to leave the key to the vault with Harold, so he can get the will?"

I look at her, she's sitting with her eyes tight closed.

"Never mind the will," I say. "If I was supposed to die on this trip it would have happened already, from aggravation." I'm trying to keep my voice normal because I can see Sophie is really terrified. "How do you like it we become such globe-trotters in our old age? Can you believe it, we're on our way to Tokyo, Japan? Like it would be Ellenville in the Catskills?"

"I wish it was Ellenville in the Catskills," she says. "I could believe we're going to get there." And then she says, "Tell me if we get off the ground at least, so I can open my eyes. And if not, goodbye."

Well, I give a look and I see we are all of a sudden in the air, maybe a mile, I don't know when it happened but everything is falling away, the airport, the ground, the people, and with it the aggravation too. I put my arm around Sophie, I say, "You can open your eyes, Mrs. Seidman, we are air-borne."

She takes a look, then she gives my hand a squeeze and suddenly, like happened so many times in my life with this woman, I am a very happy man I picked her out instead of maybe a hundred million others.

Now one of the stewardesses (did you ever see such living dolls they've got on these planes?) she gets up in front and makes a nice little speech, welcome from the company, they can say this again, I just paid them over three thousand dollars for tickets. And then she says, in case something goes wrong with the air pressure, there's free oxygen, and she pulls down from the top an oxygen mask to show how it works. Very nice. They can keep the oxygen and see that nothing goes wrong with the air pressure.

Next she says we are going to be flying over the ocean most of the way and everything is very safe, nobody should worry, but just in case, one in a million, something should happen and the plane has to go down in the water, there's a life preserver in the seat—and she gives a demonstration how it works. You put on the jacket, you tie it, you pull something or push something, to blow it up, but you're not supposed to do this until you crawl out of the window first and into the water, *then* you pull the button or push it, if you can find it. And then there's a whistle in one of the pockets, you can blow for help. And when you're in the water already and you remember to tie all the strings and blow up the jacket, and you blow the whistle already, then there's something else. In case a shark should answer the whistle instead of a rescue boat, you've got also in the jacket some shark repellent, you can shoot it out by pressing another button.

Well, by this time the lecture is not for me. Because I'll tell you the truth, if I have to land in the ocean in the middle of the night, and start blowing a whistle for help, and on top of this I've got to think about sharks, the way they are moving, fast and slow at the same time, like all the bad dreams you ever had put into one, and you're laying there in the water like a crouton, with your inflated life jacket, and the shark is turning over slow motion to take off your leg or a piece of your behind—well, if it comes to this already, I don't need any shark repellent. I am dead of heart failure and they can put me on a casualty list.

So happens it was a perfect trip, no pressure failure, no sharks. You know what a marvelous thing it is with those jets, you've been flying on them from California, it's like you would be riding on tracks in the sky and every few minutes one of the stewardesses comes with pillows, magazines, gum, cocktails, lunch, coffee, tea, more cocktails, more magazines, dinner, and I'm sitting there reading a little, eating a little, napping a little, like in my own living room, imagine, five miles in the air, hanging, and on the ground I'm a man can't look down from the second floor without getting dizzy.

You know how it says in the travel books, we arrived without incident? Well, this is how it was with us, except one little incident, at the Customs, made up for a few we didn't have. We got lucky to draw one of those officials, you find them in every country—the least maybe in Japan, anyway my experience—but you give these fellows a badge and a little authority and you are in big trouble with them, unless you've got a bigger badge and more authority. This one, I'm sure, was going to have a revenge on every American tourist, for the war, the occupation, what the GIs did to spoil the girls, everything. And to rub it in, always with the false smile and the bows.

We opened up for him all the suitcases, he makes a mishmash of everything and Sophie is getting very nervous, you know how it is, like with policemen and the income tax fellows, just the look of them, you're already guilty, you don't know what, but guilty. Well, finally there's nothing more to open up, he gives me a look, very arrogant, and he says, "You have nothing to decrare?"

I'm pretty mad by now, you understand. I say to him, "What would you like me to open up next, my head?"

And he says, wooden, every word he cuts off like with a scissors, "Have you anything to decrare, currency, contraband of any kind?"

And I say, I couldn't help myself, "I got here in my pocket a little opium for personal use, do I have to declare this?"

Sophie gave me such a poke with an umbrella, it's a wonder I didn't get an appendicitis, and the man calls over a colleague, they take me in a room and I've got to take my clothes off and I don't know what would have happened, maybe I would still be there, in jail, or maybe they would have operated on me, you know where, to see if I got hidden there a package of opium, but finally a man showed up from Ruditzky's office and he got everything straightened out in two minutes.

At the hotel we find reserved for us a beautiful suite, there's flowers and a note from Martin Ruditzky, he's one of the sons, we should get settled, look around, he'll send a car for us tomorrow, with his wife, to show us the sights, and we shouldn't plan anything for tomorrow night, we're invited for a celebration, for the old man's birthday.

Sophie was still mad at me on account of what I did at the Customs but finally I joked her out of her mood and we went down to the lobby and again we had a stroke of fortune. We ran into, first thing, a cousin of my wife, her husband made recently a lot of money in real estate and she is absolutely impossible. Not from the money, she was impossible before, but with money you've got more scope for it. She falls on us like we would be the closest friends, in New York we never see them because I can't stand them, neither her nor her husband, and now I could see she's going to hang onto us like a leech and she's got to give us the whole story about Japan. She's been here four

days and she can't stand it. What doesn't she like?
What I could figure out, mainly two things. First
of all too many of the local people speak only
Japanese, you would like to hear from them already a word of plain talk a person could understand. And second place, it's nothing like on
Central Park West.

For everything this woman has got one expression. "Who needs it?" Nikko? Who needs it?
There's better scenery in the Catskills. And with it
you can get a hot dog sometimes, or a malted, on
the road. Kabuki? Who needs those crazy voices,
they're not even speaking English? Geishas? Who
needs girls should go to school fifteen years to
learn how to serve a cup of tea? For what else they
do you don't have to take lessons. The service?
Who needs all the bowing, you can't get an extra
towel when you want? The sights? Who needs to
take off the shoes all day long so you could go into
temples where there's nothing to see anyway?
Kimonos? Who needs such sleeves to drag in the

coffee? And where in this terrible country can you get a decent cup of coffee, a fire on her husband Maurie's head, she wanted to go to Europe and he insisted on dragging her twelve thousand miles so he could lay in those baths every afternoon where there's girls to wash you, he'll end up yet with a disease from one of them.

And then she says, she's carried away already with this windfall that happened to her, running into us like this, "Let's have breakfast together tomorrow but not in the hotel, it's terrible, the food here." And she drags us over to the Information lady in the lobby and starts to have an argument with her because she doesn't know where to send us to get bagels and lox in the morning.

So I decided then and there, who needs this? I said to her, "Muriel, I figured out on the plane, it's going to cost me a fortune, this trip. Maybe a hundred dollars a day. You know, I am first of all a businessman. Doesn't make sense to me I should spend time with people over here I could see in New York for sixty cents in a taxi. So I'll tell you what. Let's skip breakfast tomorrow and I'll make a date with you, we'll meet in New York the second Tuesday in November, we'll have then our own list, everything we don't like about Japan, and we can go over it together, in detail. Meanwhile, you'll excuse us, I'm going to pick up a package of raw fish somewhere and go sit in a Japanese movie." And I take Sophie by the arm and walk away.

"You're terrible, Morris," she says, but I can see she is holding herself in not to burst out laughing.

Well, we walked around for hours. It's not a beautiful city, Tokyo, looks like a big slum actually. You can see how they are copying everything from us, and it's not necessarily such a benefit for them. Neon, for instance. I never saw so much of it, and such colors—violet, shocking pink, purple, bright blue. They are crazy for neon. I think they would wear it on their hats if they could. And pachinko. This is another craze they caught from us. Every block there's a pachinko parlor, sometimes two. It's kind of a pinball game, only they got the boards upright, so the people could stand there shoulder to shoulder and throw in the balls five times as fast. And there's such a racket coming from these places, like a dozen machine guns going at once. And always crowded, people standing there like hypnotized, throwing in the little balls, watching the boards like they were going to see there some big secret about life, how not to be lonely, or confused, or poor. And what you get, actually, if you get lucky with a big score, is a few candy bars, or some packages of gum. It's kind of sad.

And sometimes it comes out comical—their idea of our ideas. For instance, how they advertise in the restaurant windows what you can get inside, either with pictures, or models made from wax, again terrible colors, gray fried eggs and purple sausages and whipped cream made out of rubber and so on.

I made Sophie stop at a little place where they were barbecuing, looked interesting, we had a couple barbecued quails' eggs and chicken livers

and duck, they call it *yakitori* and it's delicious. I don't know why somebody doesn't think, in this country, to make a chain of *yakitori* stands instead of always the hamburgers and hot dogs. Afterwards we looked for a Japanese movie, but turned out every one was showing an American picture. On the way back to the hotel we stopped in a coffee bar and there was a television and what do you think was on the screen? A couple old friends of yours, Marshal Dillon and Chester. I'll bet you didn't know they speak very good Japanese.

We went back to the hotel and from everybody there's a smile and a sweet little voice and a bow, in the elevator, in the hall. In our room, the maid just turned down the beds and I say to her, "*Arigato gozaimasu*," I picked it up from the Pan Am booklet, and I get from the girl a "*Doitashimashite*" with a giggle behind the hand, and I turn to Sophie and I say, "Sophie, how's about I should turn over the business to Harold altogether and we'll spend the rest of our lives traveling?"

"Don't be crazy," she says. "Take a sleeping pill better." And then she says, "What time is it in New York now? I think I'd like to call home, talk to Jenny."

"In that case," I say, "I will also talk to Harold. You know, maybe it wasn't so smart, leaving with him to run the whole business. After all, he's just a kid, twenty-four—"

"Morris," she says, "you've got to make up your mind. You want to go home tomorrow or you want to spend the rest of your life traveling? Mr. Global Zobel."

🌸 Next day the young Mrs. Ruditzky came with a car to pick us up. She's an American woman, Martin met her when he was in college in the States. We did some sight-seeing, there's many interesting things to see in Tokyo but I wouldn't stop to tell you. I know you are anxious I should get to the story already about the geisha. Still I want to come to it gradually, the way it actually happened. I'm not in a hurry with it. After all, it took me fifty years to come to this situation, you could be a little patient too.

In the evening we went to Ruditzky's house. I was expecting some kind of a mansion but I found out there's no mansions left in Tokyo since the war. This looks something like the old-fashioned railroad flats, you remember, only the rooms are big and there's every few feet a gorgeous Oriental vase or a statue and behind every vase a servant. And there's a beautiful garden, but here nobody comes to listen to the insects. Like in Brooklyn they just spray the insects and serve cocktails. I wouldn't be surprised that they play pinochle too.

Actually the house belongs to the son, Martin, the father stays with him. Martin is maybe forty-two or forty-four, a nice fellow, he's still scared of his father. The old man, of course, is a lion. A little lion. Tonight is his eightieth birthday and he wants everybody should dance attendance on him, but the same time he doesn't want to be reminded he's eighty years old. He looks something like the pictures of Galileo, but the astronomy he is interested in is how high you can build a pile of money you should have to use a telescope to see the top of it.

This can be fascinating, too, don't make any mistake. He told me stories about *draydles* he worked out in the old days in Shanghai, my mouth was open, listening. But about the old man Ruditzky I'll leave this for another time. That night the whole Jewish community of Tokyo must have turned up, maybe a couple hundred people, all very substantial, lawyers, doctors, brokers, business people. The dinner was buffet style, chicken, meatballs sweet and sour, noodle pudding, cheesecake, like it would have been catered from Lindy's, and the conversation was imports, exports, tariffs and the latest American movies.

Next day, we are invited for lunch to the club. Again the same people, the same kind of talk. They had a big treat for me, smoked sturgeon, they flew it in from New York, and in the afternoon pinochle and golf, and I could see what would be if I hung around with the Ruditzkys. I might just as well go for a trip to my own club in New Jersey.

So when the old man excused himself for his afternoon nap, I got hold of Martin, his father appointed him lieutenant in charge of my case, and I tell him I'm enjoying everything very much, I appreciate the hospitality and I'm grateful, but I've got only a limited time to be away from my business, so I think I should go to the Japan Travel Bureau and see what they can fix up for me, some kind of a trip to see the country.

"But Papa told me I'm supposed to make some business contacts for you," he says. "I've got a call in for Nakamura in Osaka—"

"That's the outfit makes those gorgeous prints?"
I say. Right away I'm interested. I know the line,
you could only get it through a certain jobber in
New York and the markup is prohibitive. "Listen,
if I could make a direct connection with them,
it'll be worth the whole trip."

"Well, Nakamura owes Papa a favor," Martin
says. "I thought I'd take you down, introduce you,
spend a couple of days—"

"That's too much," I say. "I don't want to im-
pose on you, you've got your own business to at-
tend to. If you'll just give me a letter of introduc-
tion—"

"No," he says, "I'll go with you. Won't hurt me
to get away from business for a couple of days."
And he gives a look at his wife who's talking to
Sophie, a plain, plump woman, very nice, she
could have stepped out, with a shopping bag, from
any house on East Sixteenth Street in Flatbush.
"I'll try to set up a date the latter part of this week,"
he says. "I'll let you know when I've talked to
Nakamura."

Next day there's a message at the hotel, I should
stop by his office. When I come up, he sends away
his secretary and he says to me, "I've got good
news. Nakamura's set aside Wednesday to show

you his plant. And he wants you to be his guest at a geisha party Wednesday night."

"That's wonderful," I say. "Wait till I tell my wife—"

He gives me a look like I just said something feeble-minded. "I don't think you understand, Mr. Seidman. This isn't some tourist *dreck* he's arranged for you." He speaks very good English, this Martin. "There's never any women at a real geisha party. It'll be just the three of us, you and me and our host."

"But what about my wife?" I say. "I can't just leave her, floundering, in the middle of Japan—"

He gives me a smile, like he understands I just said this for the record. "My wife'll take her in charge. There's always shopping. I'll drop the magic word—nine-millimeter pearls. You won't have any trouble." He lights himself a cigar, I can see he's very pleased he can be so helpful to me. "I wouldn't necessarily say anything to her about being entertained though," he says. "As you said yourself, this could be an important business connection for you to explore. We'll take the plane down to Osaka Wednesday morning, it's a short trip. We'll plan to spend a couple of days, be back Friday or maybe Saturday."

"How long does it take, a geisha party?" I said. It's only partly a joke, actually I had then no idea except that it sounds glamorous, like the Arabian Nights, and could maybe also go on for a thousand and one nights.

"Well, we don't want to rush things," Martin says, and again he gives me this smile, like we've got here a little conspiracy going. "I don't know if Nakamura's current protégée is the one I saw a couple of years ago. But if she is, you'll see one of the loveliest products ever turned out by Japan. Strictly for home consumption. This is a big concession for Nakamura. He's old-world Japan, doesn't generally let the bars down for foreigners. You're in luck, Mr. Seidman."

He's telling me how lucky I am but I could see he's excited himself. It's interesting, how you get suddenly these glimpses into people, the relationships. This forty-odd-year-old boy, between his father and his wife I guess he's got a pretty tight rein on him, and I'm a golden opportunity for him to play hooky.

"I'd stress the business aspect of this trip with your wife," he says. "Most women, they hear *geisha,* they think it means a wild party with Japanese B-girls. It's not true, of course. These girls are the soul of refinement. Make your Wellesley product look like rawboned milkmaids."

He gets up, gives me a clap on the shoulder. "I don't know what kind of business arrangement you can work out with Nakamura," he says, "but you're way ahead already. You'll have something really to remember about Japan."

He was right, you know. In a way, I've got to be grateful to him.

I don't know if Sophie had any idea there was a little something besides business included in this trip, but Wednesday morning she's got a last-minute instruction for me. "Just don't lay around in those baths all day and night," she says. "You'll run yourself down and get something and the whole trip will be spoiled."

"I'm not going for baths," I say. "I'm going for business." Would you believe it, I feel already a little peculiar that I'm holding back from her about the geisha party. Seems so foolish, like I would be planning a big escapade. So naturally, I get annoyed with her. "What are you worried about?" I say. "You got me filled up with so many shots, I don't know what's left could get near me."

"All right," she says. "Just don't go looking. You're a grown man with a second grandchild on the way. Remember that."

Leave it to Sophie. Just in case I would want to kick up my heels a little, which I think you know me well enough it's not very likely, she's got to first take the starch out of me. All the same, I felt a little keyed up, to be honest with you. Just the idea, to be alone in the middle of Japan, it's already kind of an adventure for me. I took along a book on the plane, I thought I would read up a little about the history of the geishas, but Martin gives a look, he says it's no good, the book, it's a waste of time.

You know it's a funny thing, you can't get on

this subject in Japan the same opinion from any two people. You can understand that afterwards I made a lot of inquiries. It was very much on my mind, the whole time we were in Japan. The impression I got is they think it's somehow a reflection on the country, the entire geisha business. It's like, for instance, you would start asking here what is this American craze for big busts. From the amateur psychologists you would get oral-anal and anal-oral, and from the Left Wing you would get that our whole culture is infantile and it's got something to do with General Motors, and other people, they would deny it altogether. There's no such craze at all, they would tell you, it was invented by Madison Avenue or it's Communist propaganda, and anyway, what's wrong with liking that a woman should look like a woman, maybe you've got homosexual tendencies or something, that you're asking this question in the first place?

No, happens this is one idea I didn't have, that geishas are high-class prostitutes. What I found out since, of course, I wonder how this idea ever got around. Maybe from the GIs, every girl they picked up in a bar they called a geisha. It's like you would say Madame Pompadour and Madame du Barry were just high-class prostitutes. Although

I suppose there's people who would say this. I see now there's a whole society says President Eisenhower was a Communist. People like this, you know, you've got to give them credit. They are trying to keep the world simple, down to fundamentals. If you are a Jew you're a Shylock, if you're a Negro, you want to rape their sister, and so on. They don't want to bother their heads with confusing details.

Anyway, about geishas, I suppose you've read yourself a lot on this subject. Well, you want my opinion, it's as good now as anybody else's, the first thing you have to understand is the geisha doesn't belong in the modern world. It's like, I don't know, it's hard to give a good example, but say you would see a Pilgrim Father, with his wife in a bonnet, shopping at Saks, and it's not a masquerade but the real thing. The only thing you could say for sure about the geisha is that a Puritan maiden she's not. She is a toy figured out by those old shoguns to play with. They weren't bothered that she is a woman, with a character and a temperament, needs to love and be loved. The geishas got raised for one purpose, to entertain the lord. Like we raise chickens for all white meat.

And in the old days, if there was a crazy girl, a dybbuk got into her and she rebelled against the system, there was no problem. Off with her head. A geisha left her patron, there was no place for her to go. She could starve or she could take her lover and jump off a cliff. This is why all the old stories about geishas are tragedies.

It's inhuman, actually, but then you've got to realize, it started in a time when in Europe there was the Inquisition and they were burning heretics. The reason you could find in Japan things like this is, it's only a hundred years since they came out of the Dark Ages, bang, into modern life. And with everything else, this is going to change too, of course. I saw, in Kyoto, before we left, it was in a kind of cabaret, a few of them were sitting, like flowers arranged, with those high-shade kimonos and the headdresses, and when the band started to play you could think you are in any American night club, and these girls got up to dance with some Japanese boys, the cha cha, it looked so strange to me, I can't tell you.

I found out there's society with these girls, too. Upper class, middle class, lower class. The lowest are the ones, I suppose, that become actually prostitutes. Not because they want to but, without a patron, they've got no other way to go. You hear stories about American officers in the occupation time, sometimes business people too, lived with geishas, sometimes they got married. I don't know anybody ever met one of these couples. I could warn you this, if you go over there, thinking right away you'll meet a geisha and from then on all you have to do is take your temperature once in a while to find out how happy you are, on this assumption you could lead a very lonely life in Japan. The real thing, trained like she used to be in the old days, is kept by her patron like a jewel in a box and it's very seldom, believe me, a foreigner gets even a peek. Because this is always tied up with the high-class Japanese who are willing to do business with the foreigner and meet him sometimes for lunch or in the club for

a drink, but comes to their private life, there's a wall a mile high.

I wouldn't have had a chance, neither, except the old man Ruditzky had this Nakamura under some kind of an obligation and the Japanese, especially from the old, fine families, are very strict with themselves in this respect. An eye for an eye you could count on anywhere. But a favor for a favor, for this you've got to have a gentleman. They are not my type, the gentlemen from Japan. But they are not from Gilbert and Sullivan neither. What I'm saying, it had to be these particular circumstances, and this particular girl, and this particular man, Nakamura, to happen to me what did.

One thing more I have to tell you, it's important for the story, how it worked out. Just before we got off the plane in Osaka, Martin says to me, "I want to tell you a little about this Nakamura. He's old aristocracy, educated abroad, dresses like a London banker, but underneath there's a thousand years of shogun. Better let him set the pace about any business discussion. You'll always get further and faster anyway with the Japanese by not trying to rush things. There'll be tea and conversation and the party tonight. And then tomorrow, or next day, you'll get around to talking business."

"I understand," I say—I almost felt like saying "Sonny"—"in my day I've done business with all kinds of people. I never made a mistake yet, rushing in before it was time."

"Oh, and another thing," he says. "You'd better tell me now so there won't be any misunderstanding tonight. How do you feel about sampling the merchandise?"

Well, I get hot and cold now when I think of how stupid I was, a man my age, I didn't realize what he was talking about. "You mean he's going to bring along samples tonight?" I said. "I thought you said we've got to go slow about business."

He gives me that smile again. "Mr. Seidman," he says, "you don't have to be cagey with me. We've both been around awhile."

"Martin," I say, "I appreciate you want to guide me, I shouldn't make any bad mistakes. But you've got to leave it to me. I think I've got some judgment. I'm going to feel my way. I'll look, I'll consider, if I like what I see, it excites me, at the right time I'll make my move. With or without samples."

So he laughs, like I said something very clever, he claps me on the back and he says, "Mr. Seidman, you're a fox. I'd like to see you tangle sometime with my father."

Sure. He's such a grown man, he would like to see anybody tangle with his father. Except himself.

✿ Osaka, like Tokyo, got no special Oriental character. It's a modern city, big buildings, if there were no people in the streets and the signs were in English instead of Japanese, you could think you were in Des Moines, Iowa.

We called on Mr. Nakamura in his office. Like Martin said, I could see right away this is a very high-type man, highly educated, he speaks a beautiful English, and his manners—in two minutes you feel like you are a barbarian, your voice is too loud, and your feet are too big, and you wish you would have gone to school to know how to use your hands. You know what I mean?

First he serves us some tea—I mean a girl serves us, in a gray silk kimono with blue birds embroidered, looks like a movie starlet. Then he takes us in the factory, it covers a whole block, with all modern equipment, the latest. Then he takes us to another smaller building, he's got there a couple of geniuses working with the designs and colors, and I'm getting excited. I can see already the possibilities. "Evening Mist, for evening wear, created by Nakamura of Japan for Seidman and Son." "The Bamboo and Willow World, a collection of prints by Nakamura of Japan, exclusively styled by Seidman and Son." I could see how Harold will go to town with this stuff in *Women's Wear.* . . .

But I've got to hold myself back. I'm also curious to know where Ruditzky comes in with his *draydle,* there's got to be one with the old man, even if he wants to do me a good turn. A man like this, it's not a matter of money. It's a question of honor for him to make a profit, whatever it is. But I have to leave all this for tomorrow. Today is only to listen and exchange polite *shmoos.*

I was really very impressed with Mr. Nakamura and his whole operation. It certainly looked like this old aristocrat is no slouch when it comes to running a business. And the same time he talks to me about literature, he knows about Mark Twain, Oliver Wendell Holmes, Emerson. He knows quite a bit about our history and I'm ashamed I can't show him I know as much about Japan. But I figure nobody ever hates you if you ask them to enlighten you. So I kept asking him questions about the history, Japanese art and so on, and he could see I'm really interested, so he says he will take off the rest of the day and drive me over to Kyoto, we have to be there anyway for the geisha party, and he will show me a few things, historical. Well, I saw there more in one afternoon than I would see in a week otherwise, the Shogun's Palace, with the Kano paintings and the Katsura and the Rionji and the art shops on Shin Monzen Street—but I don't want to give you here a travelogue, some other time if you want, I've got a lot written down. For instance, you've got to be very passionate about temples to run out of them in Kyoto. There's more than four hundred. Also, if you are crazy about hard-boiled eggs, Kyoto is the place for you. You can buy them from stands, on every corner. But now I want to tell you about the party.

First of all, where the teahouse is, the name is Gion and it's a very old section, you find it mentioned in some of the old stories. I wouldn't try to describe it to you. I'll give you something to read I brought back, with pictures. Fascinating. Like you would walk into the past, step by step, hundreds of years.

We come into this teahouse, it's supposed to be also famous from the old days, and there's a delegation waiting for us, like for royalty. They take away our shoes and put slippers on the feet and they walk with us backwards to the room where we are going to eat. Everybody is trying to bow lower than everybody else. We come to the room where we leave the slippers outside and inside is a beautiful low lacquer table, with lacquer armrests, and from a window, open, you can see a little garden outside, it looks enchanting with the lights, and there's here another delegation waiting, everyone with the noses practically on the floor. There's the mama-san, she's like the chaperone, and a lady orchestra, three pieces, samisen, looks like a long skinny banjo, a sort of drum, and another instrument, they call it a biwa, looks like a mandolin and sounds like scraping a nail on the bottom of a kettle.

Then there's the maikos, they are junior geishas, maybe thirteen, fourteen years old. And the geishas, three of them, I guess one each for Martin, Nakamura and me. Mine is called O-yuki and she speaks a wonderful English but this I didn't find out right away. I think Nakamura got the idea by now that I am not a Texas type tourist, I'm only waiting, with everything he shows me, to say, "In our country we've got bigger." I'm really fascinated, and not alone fascinated, but like I've been trying to tell you, there's to me something touching, grabs my heart about these people. I don't know, is it the manners, the courtesy, the voices? Well, I think he feels this, Mr. Nakamura, and he is anxious for his part now not to give me a once-over-lightly just to pay off his obligation to Ruditzky, but to show me a real typical atmosphere of a geisha party, in the old tradition.

Anyway, this is what I think, why he didn't let me know right away that O-yuki speaks English. The room, he tells me, is copied exactly from a room we saw in the Shogun's Palace this afternoon. We put on kimonos and sit on the floor, naturally, on cushions, and right away my knees start to hurt. But with me, this evening, it is do or die, I'm going to stand it if it kills me. Martin, I see, manages fine, like he's at home in this position, but the one who gives me the feeling really I am looking at something not from my own world is Nakamura.

He is a very good-looking man in the Japanese way, high cheekbones and the shape of the eyes gives something a little cruel to the expression, but otherwise his face shows nothing. The age I couldn't tell, maybe fifty, maybe more. But he sits very straight, like in an old print, one of those lords, it's not too hard to imagine a topknot growing out of his head.

I'll try to describe to you the girls, my first impression. Each is wearing a different color kimono and sash, heavy embroidered silk, with flowers or birds, and long, it trails on the floor. I understand these outfits cost sometimes thousands of dollars. The hair is very black and shiny, arranged very elaborate, with big pins stuck in and ornaments dangling. The faces are made up with white powder, like chalk, only a little rouge on the eyelids and the bridge of the nose and a dab on the lips, so the mouth looks like a pink bud. The whole effect is peculiar, without expression, like a doll's face.

I tried to figure out why they should think this is attractive, this white mask, and I think I've got the reason. In this country everybody wants to be tanned. Why? After all, millions of people are second-class citizens because they've got dark skins. You know why? Because to be tanned is a status symbol. If you have to work in an office the whole year, and ride in the subway, and once a year you get a week or two vacation, from where are you going to get a tan? You've got to go in the winter to Florida or California and in the summer to the mountains and in between maybe for a cruise. So if you are tanned it means you've got money for these things and leisure and you are somebody. Ordinary people, workers, could only get sunburned. They come back from the vacation they're red like lobsters, or the same green as before.

In the Orient, it's just the opposite. If your skin is dark from the sun, this means you are a person who works in the fields, or a coolie or something. Only a high-class person can have a pale skin. So it's a religion they should stay out of the sun, and they put that white stuff on to make it more so, and they let the fingernails grow long, so no one should think they've got to lift a finger to make a living. And this is how it starts up a tradition.

Actually, the charm with these girls is not the face. It's the whole person, how they walk, how they sit, the voices, the hands, each movement like a flower bending in the wind. But for this you

have to get accustomed a little. At first it looks only strange.

The younger ones, the maikos, got their hair swept up on both sides like butterfly wings and when I made a comment on this to Nakamura—I want to show him I'm interested and appreciative, you understand—he says, "You are most observant, Mr. Seidman, that is, in fact, the name given to this style of headdress." And then he tells the girls, in Japanese, what I said and they applaud, like it was something very remarkable that I've got eyes in my head.

I am the guest of honor so I sit in front of the tokonoma, this is a niche where there's a beautiful scroll hanging and on a little table one flower in a vase. The geishas are sitting alongside us, on their knees, and first thing they pour out some sake, this is a rice wine and they serve it warm, it's very pleasant, and you drink it from little cups, each one is a museum piece. There's talk, compliments, jokes, Nakamura translates everything for me but I realize it's a regular game, this conversation, there's rules, like in tennis, and naturally I don't know the fine points, so a lot of it I don't get. But with the sake it's not hard to laugh, even if the jokes seem not too funny, sometimes even kind of childish.

Now comes the food—soup, fish, more soup, more fish . . . what went into my stomach that night, my mother would have had a conniption, eel and lobster and chopped-up raw fish, everything small portions, served always in beautiful dishes, so every course should make a picture. And the geishas pour the sake and every time I make a re-mark to Nakamura, how delicious the food is, and how beautiful it's served (he translates everything, back and forth, from me to the girls and from the girls to me) or I ask a question, or I manage with the chopsticks to pick up something to my mouth, they act like I would be some kind of a genius. And you know, a peculiar thing. After three cups of the sake, I am half believing it myself. Maybe this is the secret of the whole operation.

At one point, when O-yuki is talking to the mama-san, something private, Martin bends over to me and whispers, "You're really the guest of honor tonight. That's Nakamura's private stock sitting next to you. What do you think of her?"

"If I could see her, behind all that chalk," I whisper back, "I would give you an opinion."

He doesn't think this is funny. He gives a shake his head, with a frown, I should get back to being a genius and compliment everything. Finally the waitresses bring in bowls of rice with some tea and this is the end of the meal. Now each of the geishas takes a turn to perform. They accompany themselves on the samisen and sing a little song. At first, I can't help thinking, well, Galli-Curcis these girls are not. The speaking voices are lovely, high-pitched but very sweet on the ear. But the singing, seems to me I heard better music from the sewing machines in my shop. The songs sound kind of screechy and there's no tune to anything.

Then the lady orchestra gives a little concert, this sounds altogether like they would be moving around a creaky bed. Then the girls dance, first the three graduate geishas together, then with the maikos. This looks to me also not like Pavlova with her troupe but nice, charming. Then more singing, and gradually it begins to sound better, even pretty in an odd way. Of course, you understand, all the time I'm politely finishing what's in my cup and it's always getting filled up again.

Meanwhile, Nakamura is trying to explain to me the meaning of the songs and dances. It's very interesting but every once in a while his voice gets fuzzy, and after a while I get a peculiar idea that he is the narrator in some kind of a Disney fairy tale and I am the hero, a Jewish dress manufacturer who said a magic word, *Textiles,* and got turned into a Japanese prince and now it's my eightieth birthday and they're putting on for me a ballet, with flowers that got the faces of girls.

All of a sudden I'm feeling very warm and I figure to get up and go to the window for some air, but when I try, I find out somebody took away my knees and forgot to tell me about it. Well, there's a big excitement, the girls are twittering around me like birds.

"How do you feel?" Martin says.

"Fine," I say. "What's the commotion?"

"You had about a dozen cups of sake," he says. "I figured you knew your own capacity but I guess it was too much for you."

O-yuki is putting a wet towel on my head now.

"Well, she kept on pouring and pouring," I said. "I thought I was supposed to keep up, to be polite."

Martin laughs. "They're taught to fill the cups when they're empty," he says. "I'm sorry, I should have told you."

"Excuse clumsiness, please," O-yuki says. I look up at her and she wipes my face now with the towel, like I would be a baby.

"You speak English," I say, surprised. "Why didn't you tell me before?" I've been sitting with her till now like a dummy, not addressing a word to her.

"She wished to spare you," Nakamura says, "as long as possible."

Spare me. I wish my daughter would spare me *her* English and speak like this girl does. *Dig, natch, check, chop*—I had a very strong feeling just then, what a different world I'm in. But so different, you wonder how there could ever be any understanding between us at all. This Nakamura, to be polite, according his custom, has got to talk down everything—his wealth, his possessions, the meal, the wife, the children, whatever it is. Maybe the intention is the other person shouldn't feel inferior, in case he's got less. But imagine my sister Bessie would be sitting here. Couldn't you just hear how she would give this man a what-for? What does he mean, giving out these insults all the time? Who does he think he is, some kind of a god or something?

You know it's funny, you come into her house, you've got to sit and listen to how wonderful her children are, the most talented, the best marks, her husband is the best husband, her friends are the most select friends you could find in Flushing, Long Island—everything she's got is the finest and the best. Exactly the opposite, you see. And I must say, she could give you a pain in the neck sometimes, but I still prefer her way. Why is it better you should make your family, or your mistress even, feel inferior than a guest, a stranger?

"I feel shame for failure to understand," O-yuki says now. "I ask you to pardon, please."

"You?" I say. "I'm the one should be ashamed. A foreigner comes, it's up to him to inform himself the customs of a country, not the other way around."

The other girls want to know what I said and O-yuki translates for them. They nod and talk it over between them, like I just said something very deep—these girls would be great for studying the Talmud, you know?—and they turn to me for more wisdom of the ages. So I'm glad to oblige. With this much rice wine I could be a lecturer on international understanding too.

"Some places," I say, "to show that you've got good manners, you're supposed to just nibble. But I was brought up different. If I didn't finish everything on my plate, my mother would feel insulted, like it was a reflection on her cooking. Well, I took it for granted, foolishly, that it was the same thing here, with the sake."

O-yuki laughs, with the hand to the mouth. You could make a caricature on this very easy, but if the right person does it, it looks very charming. She tells the girls what I said and they clap their

hands, they're so delighted and amused it bends them to the floor like a wind. Nakamura is laughing too.

"I am happy to see you are feeling better," he says.

"I never felt bad," I say. "Only a little drunk."

The girls again want to know what I said, they have to be told now, every word. When O-yuki tells them, there's again laughter and applause. You know, it's lucky we don't have geishas in America. A person could be in big trouble from this kind of treatment. He could get to imagine he's a great wit, a brilliant talker, a regular Oscar Wilde. This is fine if you are a lord and everybody is on their knees in front of you all the time regardless, but what if you're an Elk or a Mason and you've got to go home to a wife and children who never listen to a word you say?

Nakamura is saying something now to O-yuki, in Japanese, and she turns to me and says, "I must pay forfeit for causing embarrassment to honorable guest."

"But you didn't," I say. "I caused it myself."

Before she can answer me, Nakamura says, "O-yuki insists. She is covered with shame for her clumsiness and must pay her debt."

He's got a little smile on his face. But I can see now the game's got a whip in it too. I remember what Martin said, one thousand years of shogun in a London banker's clothes. There is iron in this man. Good manners, yes. Consideration, yes. But he's always got to be the Master, no matter what.

So I figure I'll play the game a little bit myself. I say, "All right, the forfeit is O-yuki must talk only English from now on."

She puts her hands over her face and when the others find out what I said, they all giggle and cover their faces too, like I would have sentenced her to ride naked in the streets on a horse, or something.

"That is truly a grave punishment," Nakamura says. "But I fear you will suffer as well. O-yuki has attended English classes since childhood but she still leaps about in your syntax like a fish in a net."

I'm wondering if maybe he's giving me also a polite little dig here. If he says this about her syntax, what should I say about mine, after more than forty years in America? It's a peculiar thing, you know, comes to quoting somebody else who speaks grammatical, I can do it because I've got kind of a phonographic ear. But for myself, I don't know why it is, I think I have a good appreciation, even the fine points of English, but if I've got to put together a sentence with the right grammar and a good style, it's goodbye Charlie, all the sets, Shakespeare, everything.

"Mr. Nakamura," I say, "I wish I could figure out what she does with the syntax, I would make a book for American girls to study, to put some charm back into the language."

He bows to me. I don't know who represents Nakamura's line of prints in New York but I've got right now the feeling they are in big trouble if I want to take it away from them. I turn to the girl and I see she is actually blushing under the chalk. I give her a smile and I say, "It's a pretty name, O-yuki. Does it have a meaning? Or it's just a name?"

She looks down, shy. I don't know if this is still part of the act or not, but again, like with the hand to the mouth, it looks so charming you don't care. After all, you listen to a violinist who gives you pleasure with his music, he's got to practice too.

"I have name from my mother," she says. "Meaning—" she stops now to try in her mind, moving the lips a little—you know the Japanese have al-

ways trouble with l's—then she says—"Honorable Child of Moon."

"That's beautiful," I say. "And it fits you." I don't know why it fits her, but I said it.

"Geisha names are often fanciful," says Nakamura. "And they may have more than one meaning. O-yuki, for example, can mean also Honorable Snow, which in some circumstances might be even more appropriate."

He is a very subtle fellow too, this Nakamura.

Now it's time for games. The maikos play with the men something like clap hands, with a domino, and when the men miss, the girls kill themselves laughing. They're after all kids. Then the mama-san gets into the act. She pins a rolled-up piece of paper on her sash, in the back, and she will give a hundred yen to anyone who can light it with a candle. So for a half hour everybody tries, but she is so skillful, twisting and turning, nobody could even scorch the paper.

All the girls are leaping around with the little candles, trying to set fire to the mama-san, the kimono sleeves flying, all colors, they look like butterflies, with little screams, the high voices, giving each other advice. O-yuki is excited, like the rest. Without thinking she reaches for the sake bottle, she's going to pour me some, then she remembers and puts down the bottle and she looks so embarrassed, I want to laugh. She starts to say something to me, then she turns to Nakamura and speaks very fast in Japanese and I say, "O-yuki, remember the forfeit," and she turns back to me with such a comical look on her face that I've got to bust out laughing. She looks now like she would want to stamp her foot, or maybe cry, and all of a sudden, I've been looking at her all evening, now her face has got some color in it, some expression, and it hits me in the stomach, what a lovely creature this is. The shape of the face, the eyes, the mouth—really like a flower, the whole girl.

And I'm feeling now, for some reason I couldn't figure out, embarrassed. I say to her, "Excuse me, O-yuki. I am not laughing at you. It's just, in

general, I'm feeling kind of hysterical this evening. I'll tell you, I think I'll have some more sake.
If you'll drink with me. Maybe everybody. I'll
make a toast."

So she fills up the cups and I hold up mine and
say, "Here's to more laughing in the world, and
less crying," and we drink, and I remember to
leave a little in the cup now, so when I put it
down she can see, and now we laugh together,
everybody, and there's a good warm feeling in the
room, I can feel it, almost physical, like an arm
around the shoulder.

Well, it went on like this until maybe twelve
o'clock. After a while I got sleepy, I could hardly
keep my eyes open. You can have, finally, too much
of even a good thing. I figure I've got a chance to
make a deal with Nakamura tomorrow, I would
like to get a good night's sleep, be on my toes in
the morning. So I look at my watch and immedi-
ately I curse myself because, like a hawk, Nakamura is there.

"We weary you, Mr. Seidman," he says.

I give a look at Martin, I'm expecting his expression will tell me I just ruined everything with one little look at my watch. But he's smiling, talking sixty miles an hour to his geisha, in Japanese, so everything is fine. Turns out actually I did the right thing. It's up to the guest to make the first move to finish the evening. Otherwise we would sit there the whole night.

"I hope," Nakamura says, "that these poor creatures have not bored you too much with their efforts to entertain."

"I wish I could be bored like this every night," I say. "This was a marvelous treat for me, Mr. Nakamura. I couldn't thank you enough."

He bows very low, I see he is really pleased. But still he's got to keep up the game. "I apologize for our host," he says. "There was not time to prepare a proper meal. I hope you will forgive him the poverty of the menu."

"My goodness," I say, "if you are talking this way about such a banquet, I'm wondering how does the Emperor eat in your country."

The girls all got their eyes glued on me and Nakamura translates for them what I said and it's like I would have saved the best number for last.

Now I really brought down the house. I have to laugh myself, how they are carrying on. You would think grown-up men would get sick of it finally, this flattery, like children who are working on you for a lollipop. But the funny thing, you don't. And you know the secret? They really mean it, they're delighted with you. If not for your humor, or your learning, just for your good will.

Later on, in Japan, we stayed at inns at Miyanoshita, Beppu, Takamatsu, always when we left the whole staff would be out in front to say goodbye. *"Sayonara, sayonara,"* and they would look like they're ready to cry. And it's true. It's not an act. They are actually sorry to see you go. And not just because now they've got rooms to rent again. You see, life is hard for people in Japan. And short. Any minute comes an earthquake, a tidal wave, a bunch of sonofabitches, militarists, to throw them into a war. So everything's got a value. The little piece of ground, the meal, the bath, the cup of tea, with a ceremony, and the meeting too with another person, not just to brush him off, he wants something from you, or to promote him because you can get something from him. But to give him something, service, a smile, a little hospitality, a little conversation, to know from this that you yourself are somebody, a human being, for whatever little time you've got on this earth.

I don't know, maybe I'm making a fantasy. I suppose there's mother-in-laws in Japan too, and daughter-in-laws who hate them, and juvenile delinquents, and sharpers and grafters and perverts and crooks, just like everywhere else. The families that built up the great fortunes, it's a sure thing they didn't do it by being sweet and kind to everybody. They were not angels in the war, God knows, there was plenty of cruelty. Their whole history is full of cruelty, turns your stomach to read it. But seems to me this comes always from one thing. Power. From the people who've got it—or the people who want it. The rest, well maybe I just made it up, what I feel about them. It's true, I could never think about Japan now without thinking, this is the place where O-yuki lives. Anyway, true or false, I've got someplace to think about now where, seems to me, people are really people.

I start to get up now from my cushion and the girls grab me and it's good they did because both my legs are asleep and I would have gone right down to the floor again. So they know what's the matter, maybe they had the experience before

with clumsy foreigners, they start to massage my
legs, again like I would be a baby, and I'm embarrassed, I can't stand it that these charming
girls should become all of a sudden servants. Can
you imagine, for instance, you're sitting with, I
don't know, Grace Kelly, Ava Gardner, and your
foot falls asleep and she's right away down on her
knees in front of you, massaging you?

I don't want to hurt their feelings and push
them away, so I say, "Better stop, girls. I lost my
knees already. I don't also want to lose my face."

It's maybe the first actually witty remark I
made the whole evening, but this time nobody gets
it. They just think I'm cute, in general. I see O-
yuki is talking now to Nakamura, something private, he gives a nod his head and she comes to me.
She takes my arm and the other girls back away.

"You don't have to hold me, O-yuki," I say.
"I've got my legs back. I could run a mile." I turn
to Nakamura and say, "I hope some day I can return your hospitality. Although I couldn't promise
you such a marvelous evening. I'll never forget it."

He bows again, the bows are getting lower and
lower, like it would be a contest to see who can
touch his nose to the floor first. He says, "Then

perhaps—if this plain and awkward girl does not displease you—you will oblige me by escorting her home."

Can you imagine? Plain and awkward. It's getting a little ridiculous already. Like you would stand in front of the "Venus de Milo" and say, "Poor girl, she's got stumpy arms." I've got a strong temptation to tell him he should forget he's such a lord of the universe already and everybody else has to be kept in their place. I would like to say to him, "You people copied so much from us already, why don't you copy something good for a change? To pamper the women a little. Doesn't cost you anything, doesn't lower you to realize a girl, even if she's beautiful, likes to hear sometimes a compliment, it shouldn't have to come always from her mirror."

But I'm not such a big social worker I would take a chance to say this to him. I've still got a business there on Seventh Avenue, if my son didn't give it away to the creditors by now, I've still got an ax to grind with this Nakamura, and I don't want to lose the advantage I built up with him, I could feel it, the whole evening. So I just say, "This is entirely up to O-yuki. I am always glad to take a beautiful and charming young lady home."

She bows. "I am ready," she says. I swear to you I didn't have the slightest idea what a Japanese woman means when she says she is ready.

※ We go out, again the delegation walks us backwards to the front door, off with the slippers, on with the shoes, and this time I've got to do a balancing act, my knees are still not exactly in the right place. O-yuki smiles at me, holds out her hand I should steady myself. Outside, there's cars waiting. Martin walks with me to one and I figure he's going to get in with me, with his girl, but no, he says to the driver something in Japanese and to me he says, "Good night, Mr. Seidman, I'll meet you tomorrow at Nakamura's office. Better make it afternoon," he says. "About two o'clock. You'll want to sleep late." And he goes away to the next car.

Well, our car starts up, it's a big Mercedes, Japan is full of them, and from being such a brilliant conversationalist all evening, I am now sitting like a bump on a log, I can't find anything to say to this girl. The trouble is I found out she's beautiful. And I don't know why but this makes me self-conscious, like I would have found out she's royalty. No, not royalty, actually. This I would maybe have wanted to kid her a little, I know what idiots and lunatics and perverts walked around in those royal robes through the history. But to me beauty, this is the real royalty. God didn't make in the world a democracy, I'm sorry to tell you, in case you didn't know it. And I think there is built in, in every man, a feeling to kneel down in front of a really beautiful woman.

So what did I do? I fell asleep. It was too much for me, the whole evening. The next thing I know, I open my eyes, I see the car has stopped and O-yuki is sitting, smiling at me.

"Are we here?" I said. I even forgot for a minute where we were supposed to be going.

"Small journey is completed," she says, in that lovely voice, a little bit formal, makes everything sound like an occasion. Well, I'm embarrassed, I jump up, bump my head, then I get out of the car and help her out and we are in that street I told you about, with the little houses and the party lanterns, looks like something out of a fairy tale. I blinked my eyes to see maybe I'm still asleep in the car, dreaming.

"You live here?" I asked her.

"Not permanent residence," she says. "Only for festival season, in which I have honor to participate. For coming warm weather, Nakamura-san has also kindly provided house on Mount Hiei."

We walk toward the door of the house, I hear a sound and turn around and I see the car is driving away. I start to holler to the driver to stop but O-yuki says, "*Untenshu* has instructions. He will return when needed."

"You're sure you don't mind my coming in?" I say. "It must be late for you, no?"

She gives me a delightful smile. "We have saying, Time is a thief. With permission, when Seidman-san enters my house, we will close door on time."

Could you think of a sweeter way to say, you are welcome in my house? I wanted to give her a hug. Maybe if she was homelier I would have done it. But now we're at the door, there's no key, it just slides open. And before I know what she's doing, she bends down and unlaces my shoes. I'm flabber-gasted.

"O-yuki, please. I can do that myself."

But by now the shoes are off and there's a pair of slippers on my feet and I follow her into the house. It's again that wonderful Japanese style, what they do with wood and plaster and rice paper, they make poems from houses, honest to God. I can't describe to you the feeling it gives me even now, thinking about it. You could get some inkling of a religion, a philosophy—when you step into this house, you leave the shoes outside and with it the world, the dirt, the labor, the lies, the worries, everything falls away and you've got here everything you need, but not one thing more, and this makes a kind of elegance, a beauty—well, it's no use, the more I talk about it, the less I am explaining to you how it really is. You've got to go see for yourself sometime.

A servant comes in now and bows three times, once to her, once to me, and once to both of us. By now I'm doing it back, without thinking, and I kind of like it. It's a nice custom. Better than "Hi."

O-yuki says something to the maid and she bows again and goes out and O-yuki turns to me, she says, "Servant will prepare water."

"Thank you," I say. I figure she's going to make me a cup of tea, which I wouldn't mind to have, I'm thirsty now from all the fish and the wine.

"With permission, I will leave you for little time," she says. And she bows and I bow and she goes out. I look around the room and in the toko-noma is standing, besides a vase with a single flower, a little statue, I found out later it's called Amida, it's supposed to help you overcome ob-stacles. So I bowed to it also, and I laughed, I'm feeling kind of light in the head now, and the feet too, I'm moving around kind of bouncy, like I would have dropped off twenty years somewhere. You've got to understand, this whole evening, it was like in the song, enchanted. An hour ago, I was a Japanese prince from the eighteenth cen-tury. Why couldn't I also be thirty years old instead of fifty? I go to a window and slide it open. Out-side is a space that's big as a postage stamp, but what they did with it, it's a whole landscape—a mountain, a tiny forest, a rock garden, a river with a waterfall and a bridge—so beautiful, all of a sudden I've got a feeling, what a gift I've got, this life, what a fortunate man I am. Starting out in back of a poultry market, till I was sixteen years old I never got the feathers out of my nose, sometimes actually not enough to eat, and now I could afford a trip like this, my son is taking care of everything—all right maybe he'll lose me a few customers, who cares—I've got a lovely daughter, the only problem she's got is what to do with her energy, I've got a healthy wife, she's still got her looks, and we are on a wonderful vacation, in this wonderful country—I'm telling you I've got such a feeling of happiness, I'm ready to bust.

The maid comes in now, bows, she's holding a kimono and a pair of slippers. Then O-yuki comes in, she's wearing a different kimono than before, very beautiful silk but plain, not embroidered. The hair is different also, loose, and all the make-up is off the face. I could really see the girl now, the perfection, and it's like it says in the stories, took my breath away. I wouldn't forget that picture until they lay me away in the cemetery. Maybe not even then.

I sound like an old fool, ha? Well, it's going to get worse. Much worse. I don't know if you could stand it.

The maid brings over the slippers and kimono for me now, again with bows, like a ballet. I've still got nothing in my mind except that this exquisite girl is going to give me a cup of tea and I can sit for a while and look at that face. By now it seems to me very appropriate that I should put on a kimono for this, it's only the custom of the country.

Meanwhile, she's bending now to put on the slippers for me and I take her arms and say, "O-yuki, please, it doesn't fit for a beautiful girl like you to wait on me like a servant. In the restaurant, all right, this is your job. But in your house, no. It should be the other way around."

She gives me a smile, like I made a joke she doesn't really understand. The maid now takes off my jacket and starts to undo my tie.

"Never mind the tie," I say. "I can put on the kimono with the tie on."

"Hanoko has made bath ready," O-yuki says. And the maid doesn't know from anything, she starts now to unbutton my shirt. Well, finally, finally, comes down like a brick on my head what Martin was talking about when he asked me if I wanted to sample the merchandise. He was not talking about textiles, like I thought. I give you my word, until that minute—I suppose you'll think I'm the biggest fool in the world—it didn't cross my mind, not the least suspicion. And now I'm standing there, hot and cold, and I don't know what to do with my hands, or my feet, or my head, and the servant is very efficient with the buttons and I know I've got to do something, quick, in another minute I'll be naked and they'll be dunking me together in a bath.

And then from feeling so paralyzed, I'm suddenly angry. But so angry, I couldn't describe it to you. I'm shaking, I'm so mad. Seems to me that my whole life I tried to establish myself, to get for myself a position in the world, a little respect from people, dignity. Just a couple of minutes ago I was feeling like a king, and now, suddenly, somebody pushed a dirty joke in my face like a custard pie, to take away from me the whole thing and make me feel like a fool, a good-time Charlie out to get himself fixed up. By a business connection.

I push away the hands of the servant and I take O-yuki's hands, not gentle you understand, and I hold them. "Listen to me, young lady," I say, my voice has got sandpaper in it, "when I want a bath I will ask for one."

I could see she is stunned but she looks at me like she hopes this is maybe another example of wit in America and she's hoping for a funny conclusion. Hanoko is altogether in the dark. All she knows is she's got orders to give me a bath, so she gives O-yuki a puzzled look and then she's at it again, trying to undress me. O-yuki says something to her quick in Japanese and she drops her hands like she would have burned them.

"Excuse clumsiness of servant, please," O-yuki says. "Storm has come without warning." I see she is trying to make a smile on her face now, but it doesn't look like a smile. More like she would have twisted her ankle and is trying not to show it.

"Send her away," I said.

She says something to Hanoko and the woman answers her. I don't understand a word, naturally, but I know exactly what she's saying. She's scared now and she doesn't want to leave O-yuki alone

with a crazy foreigner. But O-yuki tells her again
to go, the same sweet voice, but this time it's an
order, and Hanoko gives her an unhappy look,
bows to her and goes out. Me she doesn't see any
more. You got to understand what this means for
my social standing. She wouldn't do this even with
a garbage man, to cancel him out without a bow.
But I'm not worried just then for my status in this
household.

"Now listen to me, young lady," I say. "I want
you to answer me a question." I still got hold of
her hands and she takes them away now. She's
still trying to make with her face like she would
be smiling.

"You ask question of 'young lady,' " she says.
"Does name of O-yuki no more please you?"

"All right," I say, "Miss Honorable Child of
the Moon or the Snow or whatever it is. Tell me,
when was it fixed up you should take me home? I
figure it's your home, not a bathhouse. And who
gets the bill?"

She gives up with the smile finally and she's
looking at me now like I would have slapped her
and she doesn't have the slightest idea why.

"Please to explain anger," she says. "I do not
understand. How has O-yuki offended?"

"I think you understand all right," I say.

"There's a branch of your union in America. We've got girls there too who invite strangers into their house, five minutes after they meet—"

"It is not as stranger you entered my house, Seidman-san," she says. I could hear the tears in her voice. I am not a hardhearted man but just then it's got no effect on me. I'm waiting, like a judge who's already got marked down Guilty. "Is it not so that there was laughter and good feeling between us?" she says. "That our eyes embraced—"

"Still with the floor show," I say. "Our eyes embraced. Very pretty. And the next move is to take me home and give me a bath. You don't even know my first name," I said.

Pretty foolish, ha? And cruel. This is a new role for me, to stand like with a whip in my hand, and no pity in my heart. The way I'm telling you now, I could see I must have been out of my head completely. I didn't want to listen, I didn't want to understand, I just wanted to keep slapping her with my words. And the more I'm talking, the madder I'm getting. It's like a fever. Maybe I was making up for how tongue-tied I was before, in the car.

And what does she give me back? "I have offended with salutation?" she says. "I ask pardon, please."

My God. I get hot and cold when I think of it now, how sweet—and I'm standing there, like a district attorney, hammering away, I'm going to get a conviction no matter what.

"I want you to tell your Mr. Nakamura something for me," I said. "Your boss."

"Boss?" she says, bewildered.

"Yes," I say. "The big shogun with his English clothes and his beautiful manners. I want you to tell him I don't know with whom he's had dealings from America before, but this time he's got the wrong customer. We got over there also people who do business like this, they fill you up first with food and drinks and then serve you afterwards a girl for dessert. I despise it there and I don't like it any better here. I'm sorry if I inconvenienced you with the bath. Good night and thank you for a very educational evening."

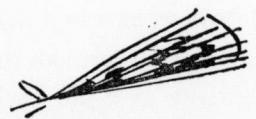

And I take my tie and coat and my hat and I go out. I give a slide the door, open and closed, the house shakes. It doesn't seem to me so elegant now, this beautiful shelter from the world. It's just a big matchbox with paper walls, could use some decent furniture, a chair a civilized person could sit on, not to wreck his knees sitting on the floor, or maybe it could just use a good strong wind to blow it away altogether.

I'm halfway into the street before I realize I'm in my stocking feet. Seems no limit how ridiculous my situation could get. Like a vaudeville act I saw once, a man is putting up a house and every time he turns around, something else falls and hits him on the head. The whole evening got suddenly turned around and I'm a comedian, a clown.

You've never been in Japan, so you don't realize my predicament, there in the street. In Italy, or in France, even if you don't know the language, you pick up just a few words, the rest with the hands, and they know a little English, you could make yourself understood. But here, every move you make, you've got to have for the taxi drivers, written out in Japanese, exactly where you want to go. And even then you get lost half the time. And if you walk away from the guide, or the interpreter, two feet, you could just as well be on Mars.

So how am I going to get now a taxi? And even if I could get one, by a miracle, how am I going to tell him what hotel I want? I don't even know the name of a hotel in Kyoto. I left the whole thing to Martin. I figured he must have made us a reservation somewhere. Never occurred to me to wonder why he didn't say anything to me about a hotel.

Why did I have to make such an exit? Now I only have to go back in and ask O-yuki to get me a hotel room and a taxi. Otherwise I got to walk around in the street all night. And maybe all day tomorrow. I could maybe walk myself to death in Kyoto without finding anyone who can talk English.

By now I feel like some fool but there's no help for it, I've got to go back to the house. I knock on the door. No answer. I slide open the door and go in. At first I don't see O-yuki, just the servant comes, and now she doesn't bow, she looks like she would like to bite me. Then I see O-yuki. She's sitting in a corner, by the tokonoma, on her knees of course, and her head is bent down and her hands over her face. And now a record starts up in my head, playing back that speech I made her, and with every word I'm getting a little sicker.

I go over to her and I say, "O-yuki." She doesn't answer, doesn't move, just sits with the hands covering her face, and it comes to me the real meaning of that expression, to lose face. I thought to myself, You sonofabitch, you are so worried for your dignity. You just took away this lovely girl's face, she can't stand anybody should look at her. And for what? Who are you, the Reverend Davidson, somebody sent for you to lecture this girl about her morals? You don't want to sleep with her, all right. So thank her politely and go. Who the hell are you, you got so outraged? Mahatma Gandhi? You bastard, I said to myself.

"O-yuki," I beg her now, "take away the hands. Let me see that beautiful face." Still she doesn't move, so I put my hands on hers and I try to take them away. At first she doesn't let me but then gently I get them away from her face. But she doesn't look at me. She keeps her head down.

"O-yuki, I'm very sorry I spoke to you so rough," I say. "I wish you would say you excuse me."

She doesn't say anything, doesn't look at me.

"Look," I say, "if it will help anything, I'll take now the bath you fixed for me."

So now she looks up, she can't help herself, the little smile, but could be she'll be crying the next minute. "Please to say how I have made angry," she says. "It was most earnest wish to please."

"My dear girl," I say, I'm ready to fall apart, believe me, "if you would know how much you please me. Maybe this is the reason I went out of my mind just now, because I'm scared how much you please me."

She doesn't understand what I'm saying and I don't understand it exactly neither. I'm just saying now what's in my heart. "O-yuki, I've got my wife here with me. Do you understand now?"

"Ah, so," she says, and her face clears up a little. "Your thoughts are with her. She is ill, may be."

"She's not ill," I say, "but she could get, all of a sudden, very ill if she would know—"

She's looking at me, I could see she is floundering again. "Look," I say, "we are in so deep, give me please a cup of tea, like I thought you were going to do in the first place, I'll collect myself a little, we'll sit and talk, maybe I could make you understand. Maybe we'll both understand each other better."

So she calls in the servant and tells her to bring tea, and we sat and talked. I can't give it to you word by word, naturally, but the gist I got in my mind, very clear. I remember, for instance, I got the idea all of a sudden that maybe I'm the first American she ever met and I asked her if she ever had before any contact with people from this country. So she told me only the nuns in the school where she learned English, some of them were Americans, but it was long ago that they came to Japan and anyhow they never talked with her any personal things, only about her studies and sometimes a question in a book she would be puzzled, but they were strict in the school and mostly it was only grammar and spelling and so on. And once, when she was a maiko, there was an entertainment at the teahouse for some American officers of the Marines and she was a little scared of them, they talked so loud and what they said she couldn't understand at all, a strange dialect. "Boy. Man. Wow. Let's go," she remembered.

I had to laugh. "You've got with me also a special case," I said, "with the dialect. I am not only an American, I am a Jew, so there's a double problem. But I want to know more about you, O-yuki. This school, how did you come to it?"

So she tells me it's a missionary school, it was established maybe fifty years ago. When her mother gave her into the geisha house, she made in the contract a provision that O-yuki's got to be sent there every morning until she's fourteen to learn English. This was because Japan lost the war and the mother figured for years the big shoguns would be MacArthur and his generals and if a girl knew English she would have a big advantage to make the right connections, high up.

It was a very shrewd judgment from the mother. The only thing, by the time O-yuki was sixteen, there was already worked out for her a contract with Nakamura. You know, the geisha houses got a big investment in these girls and they are anxious naturally to turn over the merchandise and realize their profit. Sounds terrible, to say it this way, but this is the situation. Comes from a time when girl children were sold by the parents like, I don't know, like we would sell cattle.

Nowadays it's not as bad as it sounds, actually. It's a little bit like a marriage, the contract, except that most of the time the patron has already got a wife, so this is an assistant wife. But she's got certain rights, and in these arrangements everything's got to be carried out very strict, very honorable, you lose terrible face otherwise.

The girl could choose too. She can say no if she doesn't like the man. But as a practical matter, they've got so bred into them the idea that the man is the master and for them there is only one purpose in life, to serve him and to please him, that unless he is some kind of a monster, if he can afford to pay off the geisha house and the mama-san and the geisha association and the broker, and if he puts into the contract to get her a house for five years and give her a good allowance for kimonos and servants and other expenses, the girl is only too happy to get it settled about the patron.

"What about love, O-yuki?" I asked her. "I don't see in these arrangements any place for it. You are not just a machine for singing and dancing and —" I was going to say, going to bed, but I held myself back. It was a very peculiar thing, this whole conversation.

"Is it never so, in America," she says, "that there is honorable contract between man and woman, unless blinded by love?"

And this is where we got lost in the conversation. I couldn't explain to her what I meant by being in love. Like people who are born deaf, try to describe to them the emotion of listening to beautiful music. To be *blinded* by love, this she understands. Like to be struck by lightning, or to get a fever, or go crazy. But the thing that for us, like we say, makes the wheels go round—lately, you know, I wonder sometimes is it a genuine article or did we just invent it—anyway, with O-yuki, the more I tried to explain her what it means to fall in love and it should be a quiet thing, and a happy thing, and for a lifetime, the more puzzled she looked.

I must tell you, in this connection, the mother's story, the way O-yuki told me. She was a geisha herself, she must have been very beautiful, her patron was Prince Itokari, a very influential man in the government, a minister or something. He was married, naturally, and with a family, and when the war came it didn't look good for him to be leaving the conferences and meetings to go to the teahouse to visit her, so he would send over an aide always to bring her to him, he had a separate apartment for her in his garden. This aide was a good-looking fellow, so it happened like in the old stories, they were *blinded* by love.

O-yuki told me the story altogether like she would be reading it from a book. I could tell she was enjoying it, the way the women do at a sad movie, they cry their eyes out and then say it was wonderful, they never had such an enjoyable time.

Well, one night, instead of bringing her to the Prince's palace, this young man took her away to a place in the mountains—Miyanoshita, I went there afterwards and saw the place, very beautiful, romantic—and they stayed there three weeks, nobody could find them. So naturally, there was the biggest scandal, the Prince threw her out and the

young man he gave a choice, either he could kill himself or join the kamikazes. And this is the way he died, shooting himself like a bullet at a battleship.

But you know what she says? She says, like she would be reciting the last lines of a poem, "It is beautiful to meet death in robes of fire. With honor and glory, for Nippon and Emperor."

"You really believe this?" I asked her. "It was with honor and glory?"

"My father was Japanese hero," she says. "Proud possession for my mother which misfortune take away. Proud possession for daughter also."

Can you imagine? Honor and glory. To die in flames, smashed up, a young man maybe twenty. What hope can there be for the world if people keep on believing like this?

Anyway, for the mother there was no honor and no glory. She had the baby and afterwards she tried to go back to her profession, but the teahouse where she worked before wouldn't take her in, they were afraid of the Prince, even though he was no more such a big man, since the war. So she went to another place, not so fashionable, but like O-yuki said, "Her heart was like stone, she drank always too much sake, her conversation was no more witty and it was no more joy for her to please honorable guests."

So pretty soon she was a drunk and finished as a geisha. She got married to some *shnook,* an *osobaya-san,* a noodle vender, so she shouldn't starve. And this is not a figure of speech, the way O-yuki explained it to me. She would really have starved, unless she wanted to go on the streets. But she didn't want O-yuki to grow up the daughter of a noodle peddler either, so she put her in the geisha house when she was five years old. Sold her actually, this is what it amounts to.

You would think the girl would maybe hate her mother for this. You know what goes on with the rejection business nowadays, you get such an earful about it with the kids. But she's got only sorrow for the mother, and sympathy. How could she settle to be a peddler's wife after the kind of life she had? The only way she could live with it was to stay drunk all the time with sake, until she died—an old lady of twenty-six.

"And he wouldn't lift a finger to help her, this Prince Itokari?" I said. "What kind of a monster is this?"

And here again we started to talk only words to each other. To O-yuki he is not a monster, just somebody got caught, like her mother, when the lightning struck. What else could he do but throw her out and turn his back on her? She didn't go to him and ask his permission—

"Wait a minute," I said. "You mean if she asked the permission he would give it to her? And it would be all right?"

Maybe yes, maybe no, she told me. Would depend on his mood. If he was fond of the young man, if he trusted him to be careful with his mouth, how he talked, and to remember always who was boss. But because they were *blinded* by love, they deceived him and made a public scandal and he lost face. So finished. Goodbye Charlie. This could never be forgiven.

Well, it was fascinating to me, the story, but even more so this girl's attitude, kind of a wisdom, like a much older person, or maybe only fatalism, not to make anybody a villain and not to judge them. But I wanted to come back to her and her own story with this Nakamura. The more I'm listening to her, watching her, the more I'm baffled by what happened this evening.

"O-yuki," I said, "I've got to ask you a question. Please don't get insulted, I am just trying to understand. Doesn't it bother you that your honorable patron would make this kind of <u>an arrangement for you with a stranger?</u>"

She sits, making littler the mouth, like a puzzled child.

"I'm talking about your bringing me here, to your home tonight," I say.

She puts her head down now. "Is it custom in America to speak so plainly of such matters?"

"I am trying to understand your customs, O-yuki. I can't get it through my head how a lovely girl like you could be part of this—I don't know what to call it—shenanigans."

"Shenanigans?" she says and I could hate myself that I'm not just listening and enjoying how delightful she sounds and how sweet she looks with that puzzled expression on her face, instead of again starting to put her through a third degree, like a policeman.

"Yes," I say. "You're not going to tell me this whole thing wasn't arranged, are you?"

"Please to explain meaning," she says. "May be there is custom in America I do not understand? How shall feelings of O-yuki be arranged?"

"Suppose your patron asks you."

"I have pledge to obey patron in all matters which do not dishonor or displease me," she says. "I am not servant of patron, or slave."

"Then why am I here tonight, O-yuki?" It's terrible, I know, I'm even ashamed to tell you, but I couldn't help myself. It's like a dybbuk would have got hold of me that night, the way I can't stop tormenting this girl.

Again she puts her head down. She says, "I have shame to speak so plainly."

"Force yourself," I say. "Do me a favor."

"Because honorable guest is pleasing to me," she says in that sweet voice, talking to her hands, they're folded on her knees, quiet, like resting birds. "And I think it would make happiness for me to please him."

Well, can you imagine someone would bring you a present of a million dollars in one check written out, and you wouldn't say, "Thanks," or jump in the air, but instead you would ask what time it is, maybe the bank is closed and you can't certify the check? I'm telling you, I was like demented. I said, "I'm flattered to hear it. But just suppose I wouldn't have pleased you."

She says, very straight, simple, "This would be

known to Nakamura-san. So that you do not lose face, may be I have misfortune to feel ill, must ask kindly to be excused. If companion is desired, another would be provided."

"Where would she come from? There's a line waiting?"

"Many geisha have misfortune to be without patron," she says. "May be that I too be among, one day."

Gave me a shiver. A whole new idea came into my mind suddenly. "O-yuki, tell me. It's finished between you and Nakamura?"

She looks down again at her hands. Incredible how this girl sits, so much repose, grace. I could only imagine now as I'm telling this to you how confused I was making her. To her it must have seemed that I am some kind of a lunatic, or a savage, the way I'm throwing these questions at her.

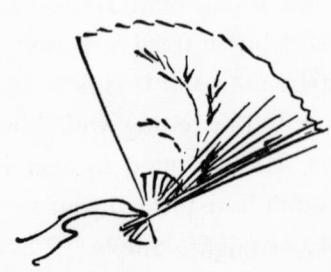

"It is not custom for geisha to question wishes of patron," she says. "I have knowledge only that it is not so often now as in beginning that Nakamura-san has wish for me to leave teahouse with him."

"So when he doesn't," I say, "it's all right with him you should leave with somebody else? You're lucky to have such a broad-minded patron."

She looks up at me now. "There is again anger in words of Seidman-san?"

"Not with you," I say. "I'm getting a picture of a lovely system here. But I'm still confused where I fit in. You are a beautiful young girl and I am old enough to be your father."

She's looking in my face now for a clue. I'm talking English but it's Greek to her. "You have not more years than Nakamura-san," she says.

"But this is your patron," I say. "He's got a claim on you. And he's got a long line of shoguns behind him. In our country too this could make a difference. But what am I—an adventure for you? Fifty years old? When I was twenty-five I was also not a catch. Why should you find me pleasing, as you say?"

She gives me a smile now, like she's relieved that I handed her suddenly a key. I am just making a poor mouth about myself to be polite or something. This style she understands.

"Does no one say in America that eyes of Seidman-san are kind and merry? And his words have much wit? And his hands are strong and gentle and they do not move more than is needful?"

Some catalogue, ha, for a lady-killer? From this you could cast a lot of movies. "And this is enough for you," I say, "that my eyes are kind and merry, and I don't bite my fingernails? Be honest, O-yuki. You won't hurt my feelings. This was Nakamura's idea, no? For business reasons."

She doesn't say anything for a minute.

"You could tell me," I say. "I'm not going to get angry any more. As a matter of fact, it will relieve my mind."

"I am troubled," she says now. "Seidman-san has asked same question before. You have doubt of sincerity?"

"I think that you are loyal to your patron," I say. "And this comes first with you. You asked me, this is what I think."

"You will pardon, please," she says. "O-yuki is not pleased with compliment. There is no honor for patron in how you think."

"I'm sorry," I say. "In America we are not diplomats. We talk plain and like to know where we stand."

"Then I must follow custom of America," she says. "You will pardon if O-yuki speaks plainly, please? Hopefully, not with rudeness."

"Go ahead," I say. "You're entitled. Even with rudeness. I haven't used kid gloves either."

She wrinkles her forehead a little, then she says, "In geisha house we know little of America. But is known to us that patron has not tender feeling for country which brings us to surrender and shame in war. Most surprising for me that Naka-mura-san makes welcome in teahouse visitor from America. When informed of occasion, first feeling is curiosity. Also little bit afraid."

I couldn't help smiling. "Account of those Marines, ha? Boy. Wow. Let's go."

She doesn't answer my smile. "Please to excuse if my words offend," she says.

"Please, O-yuki," I say. "We made up in the beginning. We are having a talk, so we can under-stand each other."

She nods, very serious. "Very pleased," she says, "to learn during evening that honorable foreigner is not rude person, not donkey, as is spoken of in geisha house, but personage of fine feelings and much wit. Most pleased with conclusion that honorable guest wishes O-yuki for companion."

I see she is blushing now but she made up her mind she is going to finish—and to give me back something for pushing her around. "May be," she says, looking at me very straight, "it is so that American girl shops for companion as for kimono? I have not counted years of honorable guest, as on fallen tree, or compared to cinema star. Is sufficient for O-yuki that he speaks to my heart. My heart answers I am ready. I have not command from honorable patron. Only kind permission to follow my heart."

Well, I've got the sense finally to feel ashamed. There's something new for me here, this kind of relationship. I'm not sure I understand it actually, and even if I did I'm not sure I would like it any better, but one thing at least I got settled in my mind and it's a big relief to me. This is a decent girl, this lovely creature, I wasn't wrong about her in the first place. In her way, and according to her own ideas, she's an honest girl, not a tramp, and she's got some spunk too. But you think this makes my dybbuk let go? No. Now suddenly I've got a new way to be out of my mind. I got a mission. A new career opened up for me. I'm going to make here in Japan a crusade. I've got to show this decent, honest girl that everything she learned is false, that what she is doing, or wanted to do with me tonight, is immoral.

I take her hand. "O-yuki," I say, and my voice got a beautiful sincerity in it, like I would be sent by the Salvation Army, "you said I spoke to your heart before. And you listened. Now I'm going to speak to your head. And I want you to listen also. This kind of thing, tonight, we got a name for it in our country. We call it <u>one-night stand.</u> It's not a nice expression and it doesn't fit for a girl like you."

She's looking at me with that sweet, serious face. "It is not nice, in America," she says, "to be happy one hour, if one may not be happy longer?"

Suddenly I don't know what to answer her. One little sentence and the rest of my lecture could go in the ash can.

"Is not true teaching," she says, "that time is nothing and beauty everything? Has lifetime of hundred years more merit than wink of firefly?"

"My dear girl," I say, kind of desperate, "people are not fireflies. They can't go winking through life. They've got to have some morals, some standards how to behave."

"How shall I do then?" she says. "I am geisha, trained to please. Since baby days it is all I learn, all I know. Now my patron has another who pleases him more—"

"You know this, O-yuki? Or you are guessing it?"

"Not need to see the wind to know it is there," she says.

"I can't believe it," I say. "Not sitting here, looking at you."

"Does not happen in America," she says, "that man tires of woman, takes another?"

"Some men," I say. "But where would Naka-mura-san find somebody more pleasing than you?"

She bows for the compliment but she doesn't give back a smile for mine. "May be need is for someone more ugly," she says. "Who can know what dreams make desires of patron?"

"Maybe he's no more a young man, O-yuki. Maybe this is the whole thing."

"It may be so," she says. "But I am young and I sleep alone more than I wish. My body is not temple but house that sometime sighs for emptiness. I am ready, in teahouse, that you be welcome companion. My heart tells me I will have happiness to please you. For little lifetime between now and tomorrow. But I will try to understand that your custom does not permit."

She gets up now. It's amazing how this girl can go in one minute from a puzzled child to a queen who just told me the audience is over.

I'm embarrassed, upset, I don't know what to say, I don't even know what to think any more, why I've been hammering away at this girl, as if to save her life, or her soul, or what. I'm feeling, actually, kind of idiotic now, you know, like once in my life somebody rubbed for me a lamp and I was dropped onto a beautiful island, everything is there for my pleasure and delight, including a hot bath, and instead of to kick off my shoes and enjoy myself I turn around my collar and start converting the natives. How did this happen to me? The last thing I want in my life is to be a Holy Joe. You know I am always saying let everybody live and be well, I am not their judge. And what is growing now in my stomach is an awful sick feeling that I just spoiled for myself a wonderful experience, happens once in a lifetime to a man. If he's lucky.

She called a taxi for me and gave the driver instructions he should take me to a certain hotel and she must have called them, because when I got there, there was a delegation waiting and I had to fight them off, *they* shouldn't give me a bath. It's a terrible thing with the Japanese, the baths.

They put me in a beautiful room and I didn't close my eyes the whole night. I got up finally, it was maybe seven o'clock, I went down and had a cup of coffee and walked around a couple of hours, then I decided I would take a chance and go out to Nakamura's plant. I got from the clerk at the hotel the address, with instructions for the taxi written out on a card, and I drove to Osaka, it's maybe thirty miles, I got there about ten o'clock.

Must be Nakamura was surprised to see me but you couldn't tell from his face anything. "Good morning, Mr. Seidman," he says.

"If I am interrupting you," I said, "I could wait."

He bows. "I was not expecting you until this afternoon," he says, "but I am at your disposal."

"I'm sorry to bust up the schedule," I say, "but I'll tell you the truth, I couldn't sleep and I was getting too nervous just to hang around till the afternoon."

"Ah so," he says, and his face still shows nothing, like it would be painted on. "Your quarters were comfortable, I trust."

"I had a very nice room," I say, "at the Miyako Hotel."

For a second I could see he's surprised, then again nothing. "It is one of our best hotels," he says. I'm telling you, what a training these high-class Japanese got. You could see how this man, if he decided, would sit himself on the floor and stick himself with a knife, the way you would cut off a fingernail. Believe me, my friend, polite-shmite, it's a lucky thing for us we won that war.

Anyway, I say to him now, "I know it's not your style, Mr. Nakamura, but I would like to get down to business with you. Plain talk. Man to man."

He bows again, maybe this time to hide the smile on his face. Like a metronome, with the bows, I could hear now what it's ticking. *Yankee barbarian. Syntax mutilator.* "As you wish, Mr. Seidman," he says.

"I am not going to put on an act," I say, "that your fabrics are so-so and maybe I could find a place for them in my line. They are gorgeous and I am very excited. If I could make with you the right deal, I figure to feature them in my style show, maybe a whole separate line of prints."

Again a bow. "I am honored by your confidence. As for myself, Mr. Ruditzky has vouched for you and—" he lets me see now a smile, pale, like a winter sun—"and I hope you will pardon the liberty, but I have also made inquiries, by cable, in New York. I see no obstacle to our making a business connection."

"Fine," I say. "Two things. An exclusive for ninety days on whatever designs I pick out for the line. Over ten thousand yards I want the jobber's discount, and I will pay for an option for six months to job the material myself in New York, if I decide."

"This is quite satisfactory," he says. "I had already planned, without any commitment from you, to give you what I believe you in America call first refusal on any new designs."

You see how confusing it is with people? In the right circumstances this man would cut my throat like a chicken. But in a business deal, he doesn't take an advantage. The opposite. "That is certainly more than fair," I say. "But I offered it already, let it be my way."

He bows. This time I bow. He bows a little lower. You know, I saw in railroad stations all over Japan this kind of performance, goes on for a half an hour, you wouldn't believe it.

"We are agreed then," he says.

"Yes," I say, and I take in a breath, because I don't mind telling you this man has got me intimidated. "Except one more thing. I understand you've got a contract with O-yuki. I would like to take it over."

For ten seconds he says nothing. In those ten seconds I went over quite a few possibilities in my mind. Will he start reciting the names of his ancestors and for each one I will get a slap in the face? Will he wait till I get back to the hotel and there'll be somebody there to stick me with a samurai sword? Or will he just kill the whole deal and tell me to get out of his office?

Finally he says, the voice has got the whole Ice Age in it, "Perhaps you would care to elaborate, Mr. Seidman."

"Just what I said." I would like to tell you my voice was calm. But it had a bigger vibrato in it than the Radio City pipe organ. "Just I would like to pay you back whatever you spent on her, and she should be free."

He's looking at me now like I would be an interesting exhibit in a museum. "This curious national passion for moving about the earth, setting people free." His voice changes, like he's talking now to a salesman he's got no more time for. "Mr. Seidman, you have appeared to me to be a man of good will. I must make allowances for the fact that you know nothing of our customs. And care less, probably. But I must ask you to end what can only be a ridiculous discussion."

"Excuse me, Mr. Nakamura," I say. "We've got a habit in America to talk direct. Maybe it's a bad habit. Maybe it's not for real that we give

a damn what goes on with other people, we are only interested in selling them things they don't need, so we can have higher dividends. Or maybe it's because other people are so mean they can't believe anybody else could have a generous heart. I don't want to make with you a panel discussion on this subject. I can just tell you that what I said now, about O-yuki, it's not a casual thing with me. I feel a very deep interest in this girl. I am worried for her future. I couldn't sleep on account of it."

He's still looking at me like he would have picked me up in a diggings somewhere. "And so you wish to set her free," he says. "You have reason to believe then that she is my slave?"

"Now just a minute, Mr. Nakamura. I didn't say this. She told me very plain that she is not your slave. You've got to understand, this is strictly my idea. She didn't make any complaints—"

"I did not need to be assured of that," he says. "O-yuki is a Japanese woman. She speaks your language but she is not a product of one of your finishing schools. She will honor me always, as I honor her."

I am getting a little desperate now, he should understand what I'm talking about. "But she is in a rotten situation," I say. "You've got to see that. Japanese or not."

"I must be excused," he says, "from seeing what you see. Or think you see. But in any case, if you have proposals that concern O-yuki's situation, it would be proper, I think, for you to discuss them with her, not with me."

"Believe it or not," I say, "I was trying to think of your customs. I thought it would maybe be more proper if I discussed with you first."

He looks at me now like I would be making him very tired. "Mr. Seidman," he says, "I will make no secret of the fact that, in the years I spent in your country, I developed little actual understanding of your countrymen or your way of life, and perhaps even less affection. If we had not lost the war you made inevitable for us—"

"*We* made inevitable?" I can't believe I heard this brilliant, educated man say this.

"Yes," he says. "By denying us our rightful spheres of influence, which you have always been careful to maintain for yourselves."

"Mr. Nakamura, you've got to be joking," I say. "You call it a sphere of influence when you march into a country and knock the people in the head and take over everything? When did we ever do this? Where?"

"You do it with your money," he says. "Which involves less risk and less honor."

"Listen," I say, "you made a deal with two gangsters, lunatics, to divide up the world. This involved honor?"

"I don't wish to debate the matter with you, Mr. Seidman," he says. "The war is over and we lost. And now we must face realities. We must do business with you. We must accept the fact that our women have been and are being hopelessly corrupted by your military and business people—"

"Corrupted," I say. "Because our boys maybe gave them the idea they are human beings, not

just toys, or servants, their whole life is only to kneel on the floor and please a man?"

"That, if you will excuse me, is not the concern of your boys. These girls must live in Japan."

"Yes, and it seems to me I read how these girls lived in Japan before our boys ever got near them."

"And now they have the magnificent privilege of wearing slacks and dancing rock and roll. Mr. Seidman," he says, "when I was in your city of New York, I walked often on a street called Park Avenue and I was struck by the large number of doctors' offices to be found there. I was given to understand that their time is largely and profitably occupied in listening to the imaginary illnesses of women who enjoy all the benefits heaped on them by the men of your country. I have read elsewhere that one out of every ten women, or perhaps five, in your country is a candidate for a mental hospital. Doesn't this suggest to you that possibly your welfare concerns would be better occupied at home?"

"When I'm home, Mr. Nakamura," I said, "I tend to my business and my family—"

"I think," he says, "that this would be an excellent idea when you are abroad as well. Since you do not seem capable of accepting hospitality on the terms on which it is offered."

By now I'm feeling very sorry that I started up this whole discussion. "Believe me," I said, "I was not looking to stick my nose into anybody's business here in Japan. But happens I'm a human being. I got a heart here, not a cash register. Happens I met this girl, I talked to her, she is a human being too—"

"Did you happen also to observe," he says, "that she is an extraordinarily lovely human being? I should have thought your time would be better occupied in discovering her charms rather than her problems. I assure you she does not distribute them carelessly."

"Mr. Nakamura," I say, "you are a civilized man. You must have some feelings. Don't you realize—what is going to be with this girl in five years, ten years—"

"Perhaps in five or ten years," he says, "your government, by its brilliant international dealings, will have made all our futures an academic matter. In any case, I am unwilling to discuss this matter with you any longer. I will say only that it was because of a sense of obligation to Mr. Ruditzky that I opened a door on my private life to an American. I have not done it before and you have given me occasion to regret it."

He is not the only one, believe me. I am feeling now like such a fool, I jumped in with this crazy proposition, that there's sweat on my face from it. "You must excuse me," I say. "I am not very clear in my head this morning. I got also a couple of doors kicked open for me, would have been better if they stayed closed. I'm a very confused man, Mr. Nakamura. In business I know what I'm doing, every minute. Comes to personal things, I am not very experienced. I could see how it must look to you, what a hell of a nerve, I accept your hospitality and I come to you afterwards with such a proposition. What I had in mind—well, doesn't matter what I had in mind. We've got a saying, maybe you heard it, the road to hell is paved with good intentions. I guess I better just apologize to you and shut up. I'm really sorry. I mean it."

So he bows. "You are very gracious, Mr. Seidman. Let us say no more about it."

"Have we still got a business deal?" I say.

"We have discussed the terms of our business agreement. I see no reason to alter them. Do you?"

"No, I just asked. I would like to shake hands on it."

So we shake hands. I had a funny feeling he couldn't wait for me to leave so he could wash his hand. Me too, I've got suddenly a fever to get away from there.

"I will leave to you," I say, "to have the lawyers draw up the papers. If there's any questions, they can reach me at the Imperial Hotel in Tokyo, next week."

He gives me a look and I decide my first idea, just to go, is again no good. "I am going to see O-yuki," I say. "With your permission."

He bows. "May I offer you my car? I was going to send it there in any case."

"Thank you. I'll take a taxi, if you don't mind to give the driver the instructions. And do me a favor, please. I would like to talk to O-yuki on the phone and ask her if it's all right I should come to see her now."

"There is no need," he says. "She will receive you. She has no other engagements."

"Please, Mr. Nakamura," I say. "You have your

customs, we have ours. Would be a fine idea for the world, instead of thinking everybody else's is crazy, just to respect them."

"I agree," he says. And bows, naturally. Then he says, "It may take a few minutes to put the call through. May I offer you a cup of tea?"

I don't know how, some kind of radar maybe, because the expression on the face still tells me nothing, I got the idea I just won some kind of a little victory for myself, maybe for America too. But I'll tell you the truth, it meant very little to me just then. I was on pins and needles while that same movie starlet in the kimono embroidered with birds came in to serve us tea. I don't know what we talked about. Politics, maybe. Probably I missed something interesting. Finally, finally, the call comes through, he picks up the phone, says something in Japanese and hands me the receiver.

"I have said," he says, "only that you wish to speak to her."

So I take the phone and I'm actually dizzy. I've got to wait a minute to catch my voice. "O-yuki," I say, "I am here in Mr. Nakamura's office and I'm saying this in front of him. You haven't been out of my mind one minute since I left you."

She doesn't say anything.

"O-yuki, is it all right if I come over now?"

"Honored guest of Nakamura-san will be most welcome," she says.

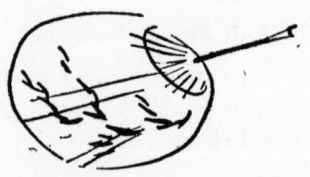

 Well, you've got reason to know I've got a pretty good memory for things. But I don't even remember getting into the taxi. I just remember that I'm standing again at the door of her house, it's like a year went by since yesterday, and I'm again dizzy, I've got to put a hand on the door to steady myself. I knock and after about another year the door slides open. I guess it was Hanoko opened but I didn't notice. All my eyes could take in was O-yuki. She's wearing a kimono I didn't see before, pale-green silk, her hair is again a different style, and I'm standing there looking at her like a dummy, I can't say a word.

O-yuki's got nothing to say neither. The Japanese got an advantage over us. When in doubt they could always bow. I started to go in, then I remembered about the shoes and I bent down to untie them, but before I could stop her she was there, doing it for me. I put on the slippers she held for me and I walked in and stood there for a minute, waiting until I could speak and my voice shouldn't shake. Finally I said, "*Kon nichiwa,* O-yuki."

She bows. "*Kon nichiwa,* Seidman-san." She gives me a smile, very charming, polite, but it doesn't tell me anything.

"O-yuki," I say, "I heard you say on the phone, Guest of Nakamura-san is welcome. Is that how it is now? Did I spoil everything when I went away last night?"

I waited for her to answer. I felt like I would be turning over a telegram in my hands, the kind you are afraid to open.

"Seidman-san has wish to know," she says finally, "if feelings of O-yuki be kept in *tansu,* like kimono? For change with each occasion?"

What I wanted to know she just told me. This was still the same girl who said to me, last night, what I couldn't take in, for the life of me, because it was so straight, so simple, so pure. *Because you please me and it would give me happiness to please you.*

"Listen," I said, "I've got to say this fast because otherwise I wouldn't say it at all. I've been married to one woman twenty-five years. I never said to any other woman in my life, 'I love you.' If I say to you now, 'I love you,' would you understand that I am not *blinded* by love, that tomorrow I will say goodbye and I wouldn't ever see you again?"

I was a little stunned, you know, that I actually got it out. And a little anxious, naturally, to see how will she take it.

"Seidman-san has better opinion of firefly this morning?" she says with a little sidewise look. . . . But then she comes over and puts her hand in mine. "It is not needful for me to understand all. Only that you do always what your heart tells to do. And that your heart beats truly."

Can you realize how strange this was for me, this situation? Like my whole life got turned upside down suddenly. Everything I believed in— responsibility, security, a plan—everything I built my world on. When I was seven years old, already I never made a move it shouldn't fit in with the plan for my life—or better I should say for my parents' life, and my sisters'. I could never buy myself a malted milk for ten cents without having a bad conscience afterwards. And now I heard myself saying, "All right, O-yuki. You used an expression last night—little lifetime. I'm asking you to make for me, until tomorrow, a little lifetime I can take back to America, to my other life."

Well, my friend, I am in pretty deep, no? You are maybe saying to yourself, going to be the same old story finally. Middle-aged fool—middle-aged if I want to give myself a little benefit of the doubt from all the vitamins I swallow and the health foods my wife stuffs down my throat—so here I am, a dress manufacturer on a holiday, I haven't got the family, or *Women's Wear,* looking over my shoulder, I came down with a big letch for a young girl and I'm just dressing it up in a lot of fancy words, it should sound better.

So maybe you're right. Maybe this is part of it, maybe it's the whole story. I'm not trying to come out of this a hero. All I could tell you, I wanted this girl like never before I wanted anything in my life. But not in a rush. With beauty. A little lifetime, not a convulsion.

She put on for me a whole new outfit. If I'll tell you it was blue, I could say the same way, an orchid is pink and the Empire State Building is high. Wouldn't tell you much. I won't even try to describe you what this girl looked like. You are the writer. Say a dream. The whole thing was a dream.

We went back to that same teahouse and we
had there a private room and everything was
served, like before, in museum pieces, but slow,
took hours for the meal, and O-yuki drank sake
with me and sang for me songs and danced for
me, and we talked and talked. What could I say
to you about that wonderful day? Enchanted?
Magic spell? You know how much they say, these
words, and how much they leave out. One time,
in my desk at the office, I counted up sixty-three
cards that show who I am in America, from the
Automobile Club to the Zenobia Nut Company
that gives me a right to buy from them on credit.

Well, the best way I could explain you maybe was that O-yuki took away from me those cards, with my connections, my credit rating, my obligations. I had no more address, no business, no future, no history, nothing. Only this girl alone with me in the world of this room. Maybe there's some women who are born loving the idea that they are women and not wanting to be anything else. They are a little out of style, I guess, maybe they're not even lucky to be like they are, in the world the way it is nowadays. But I know this, the men who touch their hearts are lucky. They got themselves elected to a very special club.

It was already dark when we went back to her house and Hanoko undressed me and then left me alone to wash myself before getting into the bath. Nobody offered to do it for me, like in all the reports you get from the three-week bachelors who go to Japan. Afterwards O-yuki joined me in the bath, it was like a small square pool but she stood at the other end, up to her neck in the water, very modest. After that, we went into the room where there were wonderful quilts piled up on the floor, *futons* they call them, and I took her in my arms and for maybe ten seconds I felt I was God, Charlemagne, even Marlon Brando. And

then I said—don't ask me why, God only knows—
I said, "How old are you, O-yuki?" and when she
answered, "Nineteen years," I said to her, like I
would be hypnotized—I swear I didn't think the
words, they came out by themselves—"My daughter Jenny is going to be eighteen next month, I
wish she could meet you," and the sentence wasn't
even finished, I knew everything else was finished,
like I would be dropped suddenly in a tub of
icewater.

How could I describe you what went through
my head in the next few seconds? What kind of a
miserable dirty trick is this? What right have children got to be such tyrants over your life? Why
am I not entitled, one time I got a chance, to
step out of my character that I got pushed into
fifty years ago? How do I know I even belong
there? Who said Morris Seidman had to be a
dress manufacturer, a family man, a lodge member always attends meetings and pays his dues and
gets stuck with the committees? Maybe I was
supposed to be a great lover. A great traveler,
like Marco Polo. A great bum, like Casanova. I
cut my life out, like one of my own patterns,
mostly account of the children. What more do I
owe them, for God's sake? What right has my

daughter got to come here now and look at me with her big eyes and spoil everything for me? What is this responsibility, all the time responsibility, like a cage, you walk into it every night with the evening paper and they let you out in the morning, so you can get to the other cage in time? Hasn't a man got a responsibility to himself, to take for himself a few hours of magic, glamour, I don't know what, before they put him away forever in a box?

But it's no use—all the raving going on inside of me, no use. Jenny's face is there, it won't go away, her eyes are on me and it's finished, finished.

Pretty funny, ha, this turn of events, like you would say in a story. And was even funnier, how all of a sudden I'm scared. Terrified. How can I explain to this girl what happened to me? She doesn't have the faintest idea, this morality that just spoiled everything for me. She is waiting for me to be her lover, like I said myself, to make a little lifetime between now and tomorrow morning—and now suddenly I don't want her. And she could start to look for a reason and maybe end up again in that corner, sitting with her hands over her face. And I will feel like a murderer the rest of my life.

A very funny situation, you look at it one way. For me, just then, it was a tragedy. Not a big one, maybe, but a tragedy just the same. I'm not fooling you, I prayed. Not to hurt her. Please, not to hurt her. Not to humiliate her again, like yesterday.

"O-yuki," I said, "listen to me. I am talking to you from my heart, that you said beats truly. I want you to listen to me with yours. You know how it is—an American businessman like me— you said yourself, I could have fixed up for me lots of girls to make love to, like we say—I don't know why, it's got nothing to do with love. From you I want something different. Maybe love. I want to remember that we spent together a day out of this world, out of my world anyway. You spent with me precious hours, like I would be a very important person in your life. You reminded me of my young days, my dreams, and this is the important thing, the wonderful thing I'm going to remember the rest of my life. Maybe, the way things are with me, it's better that this should be all of it, just to hold you in my arms like this —like you would be my daughter, but in another way. Can you understand this? What I'm saying?"

She was quiet in my arms for a minute, like she

would be thinking. And now I got to tell you a funny thing. Holding her like this, I had a feeling of sweetness deep inside me, kind of a wonderful feeling, and I knew it wasn't a lie entirely, what I just said to her. It wasn't only from desperation. Partly the words were true. Way inside me, a boy in a *bar mitzvah* suit—don't ask me how he is still hanging around there, how many times he had to get killed by now for me to keep going in this world—the same boy who wanted to play the violin, to fill up the world with beauty, he was here with me, with the dream of a beautiful girl in his arms, and he really wanted it to stay this way, pure, what a boy thinks is pure. And you know what? I envied him that the rest of me couldn't feel the same way. Only cheated.

After a while I heard her say something, soft, against my shoulder. "Seidman-san," she says. I guess I must have been a little hysterical because all of a sudden I wanted to laugh. Not a chuckle, you understand. The kind of laughing, when you start you're not sure you'll be able to stop. What a situation. Ten thousand miles from home, I'm in bed with a girl who calls me Seidman-san. Sounded so strange to my ears all at once. I couldn't tell you. Like in a crazy dream. The whole day, the way it was building up, building up, like a symphony, going to end in a tremendous climax. And then . . . nothing. A squeak on a piccolo. I'm holding this exquisite girl in my arms, trained like one of those hetaerae in ancient Greece, to bring delight to a man, and I just delivered her a valentine, like from a schoolboy, full of high sentiments. The good citizen, Seidman-san, Father of the Year, they'll give me a plaque from the PTA when I get home.

Hysterical, no? The whole thing. Some people got a talent for adventure, I guess. Looks like, with me, always got to end up a comedy.

But then she says, God bless her, "I know what is in your heart. If we have many days to spend, would be different feeling. But for small lifetime, better maybe to keep like poem, or painting in book, of beautiful encounter. I too will keep, in tokonoma of memory, gift of precious hours from gentle father that I have many times dreamed to know and serve."

Well, my friend, that's how it was. I gave her a kiss on top of her head and I said, "Listen, everything is all right, but you've got to call me something else than Seidman-san. Sounds ridiculous to me, in these circumstances." Then I thought,

What? Morris-san? Daddy-san? Better let it be Seidman-san.

So she put on a kimono and we had some tea and we talked for a while and finally she fell asleep in my arms. In the morning I opened my eyes and I remember I noticed how the light behind the sliding doors looked like an ecru lining with white seams. She was kneeling beside me on the *futons*, in that beautiful position, must have been invented by a dancer.

"*O-hi-o*," she says, means "good morning," then she said something more in Japanese, like she would be reciting, finishing with a bow.

"*O-hi-o*," I said. "And tell me what you just said, in English."

"I have need for better English to say."

Can you imagine? "Listen, O-yuki," I said, "will you forget what your Japanese lord tells you? You need better English like Shakespeare needed a collaborator. I only wish I would know how, I'd go back and teach it to a few people."

She gives me that wonderful smile of hers. Then she tries, with the lips first, silent, wrinkling the forehead, I wish I could describe you the sweetness of it, then she says, "Hopefully, sleep of my lord has been restful. Hopefully, I would be morning flower to please eyes of my lord, waking."

Well, you're a writer, find me a nice few words you would have answered her. I couldn't think of any. I was having other troubles. Don't ask me why, but I had to fight off to keep tears from coming into my eyes.

So now she claps her hands and Hanoko comes in right away, like she would have been standing by the door, waiting. She's all smiles and bows for me this morning. I was only afraid she would pick me up bodily and carry me to the bath. But she gives O-yuki a wrung-out towel, hot and with a smell like cinnamon and lemon mixed, and before I can stop her O-yuki is washing my face with it. Then she says, "Now Hanoko will bring us Japanese breakfast."

And I said, "O-yuki, I love your country, I love you, but I couldn't eat that fishy stuff in the morning. I'm sorry."

And she laughs and says, "Then we must have American breakfast."

And she puts on now a pair of slacks and a little blue jacket and ties her hair plain with a ribbon, like a schoolgirl, and we went to the Miyako Hotel and had there a fine breakfast, eggs and sausages and toast, and I must say for someone trained herself to get along on bamboo shoots flavored with radish, she ate very good.

🌸 Afterwards I said to her, "I want to talk to you about something, O-yuki. There's something I got in mind to do and I want you to be a good girl and listen, and not give me any arguments."

So she smiles and she sits with the hands folded in her lap, dutiful, but I see in her eyes she's a little worried what I'm going to say. "What is command?" she says. "Seidman-san wishes to be Japanese lord this morning?"

"I wish to talk about *your* Japanese lord," I

said. I see now the worry spreads all over her face. "You told me yesterday it's finished between you and Nakamura-san. It's true, no?"

Before I got the words out she's shaking her head, trying to stop me. "I did not say is finished," she says. "There is contract to be honored."

"But if he's got another girl, O-yuki. You said yourself—"

"That is not mine to question," she says. "As it was not for wife to question when he choose me for companion."

I felt my collar getting a little tight but I held myself in. "It's a beautiful life for a man," I said, "if you've got the temperament for it. Me, it would make me feel like a murderer."

"You must not think so of Nakamura-san," she says. "You have seen that he is person of kindness and grace and much honor."

"I know. This is why I don't know what to think any more, O-yuki, about what goes on in this country. Sensitive, wonderful people, how could they tolerate such a system—"

"Maybe," she says, "it not wise to think too much. Enough to know that it has been so always in Japan."

"Maybe not for always," I said. "What I understood from your patron, it's changing. And he doesn't like it."

"You spoke of this with Nakamura-san?"

"It's a figure of speech, we spoke. He spoke. I listened like a schoolboy. With egg on my face."

She laughs. "It is very witty, how you speak in America. With pictures." She looks serious now. "I understand feelings of Seidman-san. There is difficulty even for me to know always true meaning of patron's feeling for our times in Japan. Sometimes I feel anger in words of Nakamura-san against new ways. Sometimes laughter, but not merry. More sad than sadness. I think he has fear that old ways are passing, yet he has said, with bitterness, that enemies have used old ways of Japan to destroy us." She gives a shake her head. "Not always easy to follow thoughts of honorable patron."

"But you, O-yuki," I said. "I want to talk about you. I want to know what is going to be with you. You've got to think about it."

She gives me now her wonderful smile. "Very elegant," she says, "for geisha to have patron with power of deep thoughts. But not so good to have

herself." She puts her hand on mine. "But thoughts come sometime, like merchant with bill. I have thoughts sometime, Seidman-san, when I walk in streets of Kyoto, that I am not of this time, that O-yuki is shadow person from long ago. I see that charms of geisha, needing much study, not useful in modern time. Beautiful songs of ancestors are not of same world as noise from pachinko parlors. Story made for journey of many hours in ricksha cannot fit in time of taxi. We must keep in small world of teahouse, private, with patron and mamasan. And we cannot keep so forever. It is not only your country that brings change. Our government also wishes. Maiko must join now with others in the public school for some hours each day to learn their games, share thoughts. They speak now of baseball and cinema and television. I have heard talk of one of your cinema stars, Rock Hudson, more than of any famous hero of Japanese history."

"Well, we've got problems with the young girls in our country too," I told her. "There's only two kinds of heroes left for them. They shoot from the hips or they sing from there." I see that puzzled look coming into her eyes and I know it will take me a whole day to explain to her. "Go on with what you were saying," I say. "You think it will be finished some time with geisha?"

"I think soon," she says. "Geisha who drink cocktails and play tennis and dance cha cha and speak with knowledge of baseball contests and stocks and bonds, are no more geisha. Secretary, maybe. Or girl friend, as maiko say. Not geisha. But if O-yuki is shadow person of bygone time, can only live now as taught. I must have patron, as in old days. Whether it be Nakamura-san or another, he will wish me for bed, hopefully with high regard and fine feeling, but may be sometime without. Also for conversation and to entertain. If there be fire for some time, it will go out and I then be valued hostess for friends. That was decided when my mother gave me as child into geisha house."

"This is what I want to talk to you about," I said. "The way I see it, the whole thing comes down to a question of money. You had a big debt and somebody had to get paid off with a profit, so you had to be sold to a patron. This is an unbelievable thing in the world today. Like the Dark Ages. But I could see it was a big mistake I should think Nakamura-san would see it this way."

She looked very upset. "You spoke of this also?"

"It's all right," I said. "I realized, and I apologized. But we will do it a different way. I will give you the money and you will buy back the contract. Then he won't have any more claim on you."

She looked at me now like I would be an idiot she got fond of. "Seidman-san, what you say is not possible. It cannot be."

"Why? We talked this whole thing backwards and forwards—I didn't hear from you the whole time one word about sentiment, love, affection even—so if it's only a business deal, like any other contract, you could renegotiate. You'll give him back the money and he'll give back what he never owned anyway—you. But you wouldn't have any more obligation and you'll feel and act like a different person. You'll see."

I see she's shaking her head.

"Please, O-yuki. Let me do it. I can afford it. I can't not afford it, is what I mean to say. I wouldn't sleep otherwise, when I get home.

But she's still shaking her head and I can see I've got trouble with her. She tries to explain to me. It's true, Nakamura would maybe be relieved not to have any more the responsibility for her. But he would never admit it. This is to save her face, she shouldn't be a discarded woman. So if he doesn't say anything, then on her side she can't take it for granted that this is the way he feels, that he wants to get rid of her. And if she would come to him and say she wants to break the contract and give back the money, he would lose terrible face. Like he's not good enough to hold her, or he couldn't afford it, or something. So they both can't say anything. They've got to bow to each other and wait out the contract. Can you imagine such a situation? It's like a book I read once by a crazy Czech, Kafka.

"Listen, O-yuki," I say. My voice is loud and I realize people are looking at me in the restaurant, but I can't help myself. I'm so upset, I feel my head is lifting off. "You're a beautiful, radiant girl, nineteen years old; you can't live like—I don't know what—a call girl, a servant, to sit in the house waiting for the phone to ring, he should send you on an errand."

She answers me very quiet, and sitting up straight, kind of proud. "You mistake, Seidman-san. No need to feel sorrow for O-yuki, waiting like servant for instructions from master. I am honorable geisha, of first class. When not required by patron, teahouse have much honor if I will consent to entertain distinguished guests. I have place of honor in festivals. No time to sit at home, thinking of my condition, that I am without ardent companion."

"You've got time at night when you go home," I said, "to feel lonely. You said so yourself. And a lonely woman sometimes figures out something to do, it's not good for her, for her life."

She doesn't say anything for a minute. Then— "Is it wish of Seidman-san to take me to America?" she says.

Better she should have hit me with something. "Wish is one thing, O-yuki," I said. "What I could do is another."

"Then if we cannot move dwelling," she says, "is not helpful to try to move mountain." She gives me a smile. "We too have contract to honor, Seidman-san. Small lifetime, as agreed."

I thought of something she said to me yesterday in the teahouse. She was glad, she said, that I didn't want her to discuss business or politics. "Always most tiresome for me," she said. In school, they were always scolding her because she didn't pay more attention to these subjects. "Teachers give warning," she said, "that I must have better head for business to make good position for myself in life."

And I got a picture in my mind, just then, made me sick to think of it. One day it will be finished, the contract with Nakamura. Maybe he will be generous with her, make some provision. But whatever it is, money, some kind of business investment, for sure it will go. There will be nothing saved, no plan for the future, no security. Like she said, O-yuki has no head to make good position for herself in life. Only heart to follow, my lovely child. There will be another patron after Nakamura, maybe not so elegant or so honorable. And then another. And then, maybe, there will be no more patron. And she can go into the geisha house, to be provided, like she said, for somebody wants a little more than just singing and dancing and witty conversation.

"Isn't it possible," I said, "if you were free, that you could meet a young man and fall in love?"

I heard the words like someone else would be saying them. What a strange thing. Sitting there, talking about her contract, patron, money, talking about her life like it would be a problem I could work out with an accountant in my office.

"Sometimes I have dream," she says, "that I am blinded by love. Can never see face of companion who makes storm in my heart. Sometimes we walk in cloud, sometimes fall together in fire. Always when I wake, I have much fear."

"That's terrible," I say. "The thing I wish for most for my own daughter is to be in love all her life. And to be loved."

"I have told you story of my mother," she says, "who loved and was loved."

"That was wartime. Doesn't have to be like that."

She gives me that beautiful smile, got always room in it for a little sadness. "May be geisha live always in wartime." I guess she must have seen something in my face, a reaction, because she put a hand over mine on the table. "Must not make pain for Seidman-san if I speak so. My life is not sad, truly. I am pleased with position, with many kimono and jewels. Patron is most generous, makes possible, without request, that O-yuki walks always with pride among other geisha. It makes me much pleasure to sing and dance. When festivals come there is much laughter and good feeling. What is left I must accept. See, I make you portrait of my life. You have seen that patron must be personage of wealth. It must be so, my kimono have value more than wardrobe of cinema star. Seidman-san surely has knowledge that gaining of wealth requires much time. So patron can be no longer young. He will have family and wife. He will not leave them for me. It is not honorable that he do so. If he is young and has his wealth without labor, because he is of great family, then his marriage is long arranged, since when he was born, maybe before. And even if he has wish to break contract and dishonor great family, could not be for such as me. I am not enough beautiful, or accomplished."

"You are beautiful enough for the Emperor," I say, "more beautiful than that girl the young Prince married."

"Seidman-san must take care with compliments," she said, "like sake, not to make O-yuki drunk. There is danger, for Japanese girl, to grow accustomed. As to young Prince, he has married with one of lesser family, against custom, and this is new thing in Japan. May be will come, with such example, more feeling to change old ways, but not for geisha, I think. Not easy for custom to change. Even if possible that young man of exalted station will break his marriage contract made with his birth, to marry with me, would not be kind gift from Amida. His family would not forgive. There would be no path for us to walk, no way for us to live, except as beggars or as animals in the fields. I could not wish such condition

for noble young man. Or for myself. Unless I wish
to dream, like geisha from olden time, to die
beautifully, hand in hand, with great prince, having misfortune to be blinded by love."

Can you understand how she is making me feel
with this talk? "Couldn't you dream," I say, "that
you should meet somebody, not from a great
family, not rich, just a young man who's got his
health and a job? And you'll fall in love and marry
him and have children and a good life—"

"That is least possible of everything," she says.
"My world is geisha house and teahouse preferred
by patron. Even if I have ardent wish to meet
young man of such description, how is meeting
possible? He will not have yen enough to enter
for cup of tea. And think, Seidman-san, I have
studied all my years how to dress myself in fine
kimono and spend many hours on arrangement
of my hair—how should I live in one kimono of
cotton, with geta for my feet? How should I be
housewife? I could not sing and dance at feasts of
fish heads. I would sigh and drink too much sake,
surely, and I would fail in housework and young
husband would tire of my bad arranging and leave
me and again would be disaster, as it was for my
mother. No," she says, "we can do nothing to
change situation. We must leave as before." And

then she smiles at me, different, so I should know she's making a joke. "Maybe I keep hope that this young man, of great promise, comes from America where everything is possible, even that geisha becomes honorable housewife, with electric kitchen."

"All right," I say. "I'll go to work on it, as soon as I get home. I will find you a strong, handsome young American, with an electric kitchen."

She laughs. "I will wait," she says, "and I will make offering to Kwannon that when he arrives he will be also beautiful within, like you."

Well, you know, if you are training a lifetime how to please a man, to say the right thing becomes second nature. Still and all, she said it. I got a lot of knocks in my life. But I'm willing to say the accounts are balanced.

"So you won't let me do what I want?" I say.

She shakes her head, then she gets on her face a mischievous look, like a kid. "Is it true, Seidman-san," she says, "as I have heard, that in America men who have night of pleasure, leave money on table, as one leaves money for merchandise, and then go on tiptoe away, as if in pretend that they have stolen what they paid for?"

I laughed. "I guess it's true," I said. "I never had the experience."

"We too accept gifts from admirers," she said. "We call 'honorable flowers.' You may make such a gift to me, if you wish."

"Anything," I say. "Whatever you want. Will make me very happy, O-yuki."

"It would please me," she says, "to have toasting machine, of American manufacture, that is automatic."

"What kind of a present is that?" I said. "Anybody could give you a toaster—you could buy one yourself—"

She takes my hand and bends forward her face, close to mine, like a little girl. "I wish it to be gift only from Seidman-san," she says. "I will keep in special place—"

"Will be very interesting," I said, "to see how this will look in a tokonoma."

She smiles. "I will keep for mornings when I am alone and I wish to eat breakfast as we do now and feel, like wink of firefly, presence of friend in America who has taught me meaning of beautiful English word . . . *loving*."

❧ Well, you thought maybe with this lacquer box there was a story? So now you've got the story. Kind of a peculiar ending, I suppose—a girl is sitting in Japan putting some butter on a piece of

toast and thinking about me, and I am every once in a while putting a tea cake in my mouth and thinking about her.

The toaster? You want to hear about the toaster too? Well, when I went up to my room at the Miyako, I found there a message from Martin I should call him at Nakamura's office. So I did and they gave me there a number where I could reach him.

"What happened to you?" he says. "I thought we were going to meet two o'clock yesterday at Nakamura's."

"Were you there?" I ask him.

"Of course I was there. Where were you?"

"Nakamura didn't tell you anything?"

"He just said you'd been in earlier and you'd made a deal and he said I might be able to reach you at the Miyako Hotel. What's going on? I called you there maybe six times."

"I'm sorry," I say. "I was doing a little shopping for the missus."

"Uh huh," he says. "Listen, talking about the missus, we've got to synchronize our watches about getting back. You want to stay over another night?"

"No!" I say. "I'm going to leave it with the lawyers to conclude with Nakamura. I want to get back to Tokyo. It's enough already."

"All right," he says. "I'll meet you at the airport. We'll catch the one-o'clock plane."

I see on the plane he gives me every once in a while a funny look, like he would be wondering what went on. But he doesn't ask me anything. I guess he doesn't want I should ask him anything either.

When we're driving from the airport to the hotel, I ask him where could I buy a toaster, a good one.

"Why buy toasters in Japan?" he says. "The best ones we import from America."

"I need a toaster," I say. "Where can I get one?"

"Well," he says, "I'll try to pick one up for you wholesale."

"Never mind wholesale," I say. "I want to get it now. Today"

So he says, "Takashimaya. They've got a full line of electrical appliances."

I find a toaster at Takashimaya, a GE, new model, I give the salesgirl the address and the money, I give her extra to send it special delivery, airmail, and when I turn away to go, Sophie is standing there.

"Morris," she says. "I thought it was you. What are you doing here? When did you get back?"

"Just now. I called the hotel. Where's Mrs. Ruditzky?"

"In the doll department, waiting for me. What did you buy?"

"A toaster," I said. "For Harold. I thought I would send him."

"A toaster," she says. "You're going to send Harold a toaster? From Japan?"

"Why not?" I say. And I say to the salesgirl, "You'll send it right out, please."

And the salesgirl says, "Yes, sir." And she hands me a receipt. "Wirr be derriverred tomorrow."

"That's very fast service to America," Sophie says. "What rocket is it going on?"

"All right," I say, "it's not going to America. It's for a secretary at Nakamura's. She was very helpful. I just didn't want to start up a big discussion with you."

"Ah ha," she says. "And where is Mr. Ruditzky? He's maybe in another department buying a tricycle for another secretary?"

"Don't be so smart," I say.

"I never saw anybody so anxious to help somebody else make a business deal."

"Happens some people know what it means to be hospitable," I say. "What did you do with yourself?"

"Nothing. I bought some pearls."

"How much?"

"Don't you want to see them first?"

"Ruditzky got them for you? The old man?"

"Yes. He sent me to a place."

"Then I don't have to see them. You got a bargain."

"I hope so. They're nine millimeter. A little over."

"Did you pay cash?" I said. "Or Ruditzky wants you to get for him in exchange a carload of hump hairpins when we get back to America?"

"What are you talking about?"

"Nothing."

We walk a few steps, she says, "How was the geisha party?"

I give her a look. "You brought your private eye over to Japan to keep tabs on me?"

"Don't flatter yourself," she says.

"Who told you there was a geisha party?"

"Wasn't there?"

"You think that's all Mr. Nakamura's got to do? Geisha parties for all the customers?"

"Well, I'm sorry. That's what the secretary said."

"What secretary?"

"The one you just got a toaster for, I suppose. The helpful one."

"Sophie, maybe you'll stop playing games, tell me what you're talking about?"

"Helen Ruditzky tried to reach Martin at Nakamura's office Wednesday afternoon. There was an important call from his Hong Kong office. That's what they told her. That you'd all gone to a geisha party with Mr. Nakamura."

"Well, you want to call it a geisha party—we went to dinner and there were some geishas there, to entertain. Is this an unusual thing in Japan?"

"I don't know, Morris. You were there. Was it unusual?"

"What is this, Sophie? Some kind of an affidavit I got to fill out? All right. I went to a geisha party. What's the next question?"

"I don't mind," she says. "Why do you have to make such a big secret of it? How was it?"

"Very nice," I say.

"This is all you've got to say about it?"

"What do you want me to say? It was very nice. Very interesting."

"Are the girls pretty?"

"So-so. One of them wore glasses. But she had a nice voice."

"Morris," she says to me, "I wear glasses too. Sometimes. And I take them off sometimes."

"Sophie, what do you want to know? Ask me plain out."

"Nothing," she says. "I just wanted to know if you had a good time. Did you make your deal?"

"Yes. Maybe it will pay for your pearls. So stop with the questionnaire, please. And listen, don't make any arrangements with Helen Ruditzky for tonight. I've been away three days. I want to spend a little time with you. Alone."

She gives my arm a squeeze. "I'll wear my pearls," she says. "Wait till you see. They're gorgeous."

❧ Well, I guess I wore you out, ha? No, I feel fine. I'm glad I told you. I'm glad I could talk about it finally. You're ready for a drink, I got here a regular bar, anything you want, even

Alka-Seltzer for afterwards. You'd rather have a cup of Japanese tea? You mean I made a convert? It's no trouble, I'm only too glad. I make it for myself all the time.

I wish you could see how they do it there, the tea ceremony. They got schools where they teach it. I'm not fooling, you could study it for years, all the little refinements. Like I told you, it's a different conception of life. It says a lot about your whole attitude if you will sit for an hour for a cup of tea, with a whole philosophy and a history and even religion in it, or if you only got time to stand at a counter and holler, Give me a Coke and a Swiss on rye, hey, I'm in a hurry. And at night with the TV dinner.

Listen, you know I love this country, I don't have to prove this to you. But we could learn sometimes something from others, their ideas, how they live. The sad thing is they are learning instead from us, just the things they don't need.

Do I hear from her? We keep in touch. I'm still looking for that eligible young man with an electric kitchen. Yes, a swimming pool would be all right too. Nothing wrong with a swimming pool, basically. It's only how much you pay for it, and you know what I mean, not just money. Well, you could file your application, I'll think about it. And better put in everything, don't be modest. Because this much I'll tell you, he's going to have to be somebody, believe me.

About the Author

Born in New York City, educated in the schools and the University of Chicago, Elick Moll eventually made his way to the West Coast. There he is known as a successful writer for magazines, television, and motion pictures. Mr. Seidman and the Geisha *is his fourth published novel.* Seidman and Son, *originally written as a novelette and subsequently for television's "Playhouse 90," was published in 1958 and became an immediate best seller and book-club selection both here and abroad. A stage version has been scheduled for Broadway by the Theatre Guild.* Mr. Seidman and the Geisha, *a continuation of Mr. Seidman's adventures, was inspired by a trip Mr. and Mrs. Moll took to Japan.*

Elick Moll was trained in Chicago as a concert pianist but was forced to give up his career because of trouble with his eyes. Of this he says, "It seemed a misfortune then, but I've had the sense to become grateful. Now when I listen to Horowitz or Rubinstein I think about tuning my piano instead of smashing it."